About the Author

Paul Wojnicki spent three seasons working at Butlins, Skegness. During this time he was too busy drinking, fornicating and applying various lotions and potions for STD's and skin diseases to actually write about his experiences. He holds a degree in Literature and Creative Writing from the Open University and now lives in Leeds, where he divides his time between his three great passions: drinking, fornicating and applying various lotions and potions for STD's and skin diseases.

He also writes occasionally.

Never Mind the Redcoats

A Butlins Novel

Paul Wojnicki

'I was looking for a job and then I found a job and heaven knows I'm miserable now.'

Morrissey.

Dedicated to the good ship Butlins and all that sailed in her.

All characters in this book are entirely fictional. Any resemblance to persons alive or dead is purely coincidental.

Chapter 1

I woke up as usual, in a great deal of pain and with my daily morning dilemma. I was too ill to move, yet I urgently needed a drink. My tongue probed the inside of my arid mouth for a drop of moisture but it was no good. I groaned and climbed out of bed. From the room next door I could hear the sound of two people snoring in dreadful harmony. My roommate Craig, The Beastmaster, had no doubt pulled some disgusting old hag. I loped over to the sink, where I noticed two plates, unwashed. Empty cartons of Chinese food were propping open the lid of our pedal bin. Hmm, someone had a nice meal last night.

I poured myself a glass of water and sat on the couch as I gulped it down. Aha, a pack of cigarettes lay on the upturned box we used as a coffee table. Empty. Shit, but what was this? An ashtray full of butts. I recalled having a pack of *Rizla* somewhere in my room. I dug them out and went back to the coffee table. Working the last of the tobacco into my skins I wondered why that bastard had decided to blow a significant portion of his meagre income on a takeaway meal. No doubt he was skint now and would have to spend the rest of the week looking for unattended or half finished beers.

Minesweeping.

I opened the fridge, hoping to find a third plate. Maybe they had left some for me, then, refrigerated it when I hadn't returned. No, nothing, not even any fried rice. I scoured the kitchen looking for food but all was had it had been the previous evening: A sack of spuds with huge, tentacle-like roots growing from them and a handful of margarine portions. There was nothing for it then, I would have to brave the staff canteen.

I toyed with the idea of having a bath first, but couldn't be bothered to wait the half hour or so it would take it to fill above bollock level. The brown stream of water that pissed from those taps was weaker than an old man trying to urinate with a bladder problem.

Instead I dug out my cleanest, dirty shirt and pants, sprayed my socks with a liberal quantity of my roommate's fake *Cool Water* (procured from the nearby market) and headed in the direction of that Michelin starred bistro, the staff canteen.

'Whisky,' I heard a voice calling me as I stepped out of my *shed* into the bleak grey day.

'Oh, hi Sweeney,' I replied.

Steve Sweeney had worked at Butlins for three years when I got there. He was a tall guy, about six feet four and built like a rhino compared to the average team member. Most of the blokes here were underweight, due to the lack of nutrition in the gruel we were fed. Meal times were regimental and those of us that worked nights would inevitably miss breakfast, and lunch too if it had been a good night. What's more we weren't about to waste our spartan earnings on food. Not a chance, we had more important things to feed than hunger. But Sweeney was different; he always had cash, lots of it. He always carried it around in a roll, from which he would peel notes. For some this would have been a risky business, given the high level of criminal activity on camp. But Sweeney feared no one, no one on camp anyway.

'Are we still on for tonight?' I asked him.

'Of course,' he replied 'come round about eight.'

'Yeah, any ladies coming?'

'A couple of chalet monsters.'

This was the unkind phrase used to describe the girls that cleaned the chalets, who were to be fair, for the most part, monsters.

'Uggh, what you doing associating with chalet monsters?'

'You should see this one though mate, absolutely stunning. Fuck knows what she doing working as a chalet monster. The other one's rank mind, but that won't stop The Beastmaster, will it?'

'It'll probably encourage the dirty bastard. I'm off for lunch anyway. You coming?'

'Yeah, I'll come with you.'

We walked under the tunnel separating the staff lodgings from the main camp. From there we followed the road that led to the canteen and entered. There was only a small queue but the place was busy. Being Tuesday there were a number of black eyes in there.

'Look at these losers,' Sweeney stated. 'They get their pay on Mondays, get pissed, have a fight and, if they're not sacked the next day, they're skint again for another six days.'

It was true; we got paid (in cash) on Monday. That meant the fights, the black eyes and the Tuesday sackings. You could be fired for all manner of reasons at Butlins: Fighting, smoking pot and smuggling holidaymakers into your chalet were the favourite ways to go. I'm not entirely sure why you couldn't have guests around. Perhaps the company didn't want them to see how we were housed.

'Fucking losers,' Sweeney reiterated as we placed our rations down at a dirty table.

I watched him as he ate his corned beef hash, he held everyone in here in such low regard. That probably included me but I didn't care. He was funny to be around, they all were. This place was full of life, fifteen hundred young people living in one another's pockets. The place was rife with drugs, STD's and violence. Oh and it was also a holiday camp.

When he had finished his meal, Sweeney sat back in his chair and surveyed the canteen, shaking his head in antipathy at the occupants.

'Why does everyone on camp smoke Mayfair's?' he asked, noting the assortment of dark blue cigarette boxes sitting on almost every occupied table.

'Christ Sweeney, you're not in a gentleman's club,' I said. 'This is Butlins mate.'

'But for the sake of a few pence, why not buy a decent cigarette? Personally, I would rather quit smoking than be seen with a Mayfair box.'

'You're a snob, you know that don't you.'

'I'd much rather be a snob, than reduce myself to the level of these fucking animals. Oh god, speaking of animals here comes bloody Scary.'

Paul Carey, or Scary Carey was another big guy. A huge, beast of a man, in fact, whose only weakness was his own neurosis. If you come from a long line of paranoiacs, as Scary did, certain pursuits should be deemed off-limits. One such activity not to be recommended is the consumption of large amounts of psychosis inducing narcotics. But would he be told? Would he fuck!

I could tell as he approached our table that he was in a bad way, twitching nervously the way he was. He almost dropped his plate twice as his left arm gave what appeared to be an involuntary spasm.

'Whisky, Sweeney,' he greeted us.

'Scary,' I replied. Sweeney said nothing, despite the fact he shared a chalet with Carey.

'I've decided,' he announced, 'that I am going to put in for a transfer. It occurred to me this morning that The Broadway is not a safe place to work.'

Oh god, what now, I thought. I knew what Mr Carey was like. He saw danger everywhere, his latest fear being the mercury fillings in his teeth, which he was convinced was the cause of his panic attacks and involuntary twitching.

'So what's not safe about The Broadway?' I enquired.

'Well, for a start it's above this place.' He was talking of course about the staff canteen in which we were currently dining.

'What's so bad about that then?' Sweeney asked, yawning.

'What's so bad about that! This place is a fucking fire waiting to happen. And when this place gets razed to the ground, I for one, don't want to be working in the venue above it.'

'What makes you think it's a fire hazard?'

'The fucking staff, that's what! This whole camp is full of thieves, druggies, pushers, and losers who couldn't get a job in the outside world. Yet they are still deemed suitable to serve holidaymakers at Butlins. I'm right yes?'

He had a point; the camp was full of such miscreants. I'm quite sure there would have been pimps and prostitutes too, had it not been for the fact that sexual activity on camp was something akin to that of a sixties' hippie commune.

'Yes, you are, but how does that make this place a fire hazard?' I asked.

'Think about it. Where do the management put the worst of these fuckers? Away from the customers, in the staff canteen. The guys who just made your corned beef hash are basically the rejects from the interview stage. Look around you guys. Look at that one over there with the peg-leg.'

'You're not suggesting that a false leg makes someone a fire hazard are you?' I enquired.

'Look, it's not the fucking plastic leg that's the problem. It's the patch on his eye and the inane grin that worries me. I mean, if you only had one leg and a patch on your eye, would you be grinning? I think not.'

'Ah, he's all right, I've spoken to him once or twice it's not like he's a pyromaniac or…'

'SSHHH. Did you hear that?'

'Hear what?'

'In the kitchen. I just heard someone saying FUCK FUCK!'

'Probably just burnt himself.'

'Bollocks, burnt himself. Tourrettes Syndrome more like.'

'So.'

'So if you can't stop yourself swearing, who is to say you can't stop yourself torching a building?'

'So where you gonna request a transfer to?'

'The outdoor pool bar, plenty of fanny around there, fresh air too.'

Fresh air, I thought. This was a guy who threatened to leave camp when they made the staff canteen non-smoking. Not only that, but when he wasn't smoking cheap cigarettes, he was clutching a bong over the bath.

'Anyway I'm putting in for that transfer.'

'You do that mate, and good luck to you. I better get off I'm due at work in five minutes.'

Chapter 2

Leaving the canteen, I headed straight for Funsplash, the camp's indoor pool complex. The wall of noise hit me as I entered. Children screamed and lifeguards blew whistles like they were at some sort of rave, as they struggled to stop the kids from running, splashing and bombing.

Above the cocktail of noise, piss and chlorine, sat an ice cream parlour called Tipitina's. From where Dale Fortune purveyed ice lollies, cold drinks and Cornetto's to the thirsty patrons. As I made my way up the stairs I caught sight of him. A flurry of activity took place within the ice cream parlour, when he saw the blue jacket that marked me out as a supervisor approaching. Eventually, squinting, Dale realised that it was only me. I waved, to signal that I was alone, and Dale plonked his tall, wiry frame back on the chest freezer. His dark, gypsy-like features were contorted with pain; he had no doubt been nursing a hangover.

As I approached the stall, Dale jumped back up again, looked shiftily around and then dug a twenty-pound note from his sock. He handed me the note and I put it in my shirt pocket.

'Not bad mate, you must have been busy,' I noted.

'Not really, I've only sold about six Fab bars.'

'So, what's with the twenty quid?'

'It's OK mate, I'll make it up by five o' clock'

'And what if Lorraine does a spot check on your till in the meantime?'

'I'll just tell her I sent one of the lifeguards over to you to get some change.'

'Hmm, you know I prefer it when you make the money first. It's simpler that way, less pressure, less chance of getting caught.'

Most people on camp were on the take in some way or another. Mainly from charging customers full price, while under-ringing items, and keeping the excess for themselves. In Tipitina's it was made all the more simple by the fact that most lollies cost fifty pence or one pound. Therefore if a family of four bought four Fab lollies, Dale would charge them two pound, but only ring in one Fab thereby having one pound fifty left in the till for himself. It wasn't good to push it, so twenty quid was the limit we stuck to for one day.

'Ok', Dale said, 'give us the twenty quid back then, just in case.'

'I'll be back at around quarter past five to cash the till up,' I informed him as I handed back the twenty quid.

'Ok mate, see you later.'

'Before I go, just move your till back a bit by about two inches.'

'Why?'

'So that that light above you beams onto the digital display, and your customers won't notice that you are robbing the till.'

'Ah, clever bastard. Always thinking, that's you.'

'Always thinking,' I repeated, tapping my temple, as I turned and left.

Dale was OK but he was a liability. People were caught everyday on this camp, doing exactly the same as us. You had to stay one step ahead and never, under any circumstances, tell anybody what you were doing. Most of all never involve the customer in the scam, as a few people did. I knew one guy who, when taking a large order of drinks, would say to the customer 'just call it a fiver mate'. The punter would usually be delighted with such a turn of events, not even caring that the fiver went straight into the barman's pocket. Then one day he did this with an off duty manager from another department. Game over for that fella. Just another Butlins' sacking.

I knew one day I would become another sacking, but was determined that it would not be until after the Club 18-30's reunion, just four short months away. In fact I was thinking about cutting my losses with Dale and leaving him to his own devices in Tipitina's, so that when he got caught, and he would, he didn't haul me down with him.

As I exited Funsplash, I noted that the perpetual clouds that gathered over camp had actually parted and the sun was beaming down. In this rare shower of light the place looked slightly less scabrous than usual, not exactly glowing but certainly less uninviting than normal. In front of me were a couple of female redcoats, in uniform, called Lindsey and Sarah.

In a buoyant mood, due to the rare display of sunlight I said, 'Hi' but the greeting went unanswered. They just turned their heads and carried on walking. The message was clear, they had no time for flunkies, so much for the famous smiles.

I passed through the tunnel, to the other side of camp and approached my venue Bogart's. This was the food outlet of a larger venue called Rick's Place, which also doubled up as the staff club after ten o' clock in the evening, and was the scene of most of the camp's pugilistic proceedings. Unlocking the doors, I noted that the clouds had once again regrouped and were casting ominous shadows over the camp. I entered the building, turned the gas on, did a rudimentary safe-check and retired to my office to wait for the staff.

First in, as always, was Andy the chef. At around five and a half feet and with a blotchy complexion that gave one the feeling that he had just been attacked by a swarm of killer bees; he didn't have much going for him, looks wise. His jam jar bottom glasses added to his comical appearance and his claim to fame was that he had actually come second in a Milky Bar kid contest when he was ten. He was quite possibly the only person that was not getting laid on camp, aside, of course, from the assemblage of umpa-lumpa's that toiled in the staff canteen.

Despite his obvious failings, Andy was at Butlins to get himself laid, though not in any conventional way. He was saving his weekly wages, all seventy-six pounds of it to buy himself a Filipino woman from a mail order bride catalogue that he had obtained from what he eloquently described as a 'twat mag'.

It was possible, for anyone prepared to live like a monk, to save your entire wage. We had no rent to pay, or gas, water, council tax, TV licence etc. Provided you were able to wake up in time for the regimental meal times, you wouldn't even have to buy food.

Andy was actually quite resourceful, he may have looked like a twat, but he was still a Geordie. He had no intention of living such an empty existence. He smoked and drank like a bastard, but never actually paid for anything, in fact he got paid while getting pissed. He achieved this astounding feat by minesweeping, a pursuit that Andy had down to a fine art.

He worked overtime shifts as a glass collector in The Showboat, and would simply get smashed on other people's leftovers. For cigarettes he would often pop round to 'borrow' dozens of people's ashtrays on a Tuesday morning, often screaming at them: 'NO! DON'T EMPTY IT' and these 'dimps' would see him through the week ahead. He was, in short, a bum, but a bum with income. And no one except Mail Order Brides Monthly was going to part him from that income.

There was a very good reason that Andy worked the same shifts as me, and that reason was his physical appearance. As section leader, and therefore being the one in charge of the venue's staff rotas, I had a simple formula. Any good-looking female staff worked the same shifts as I did; any good-looking male staff (i.e. the competition) worked the opposite shift, or even better on the ridiculous-looking hot dog bike; make them look a cunt. This was, of course, an unofficial rule, but by the same token it was the reason that Dale worked in Tipitina's rather than Bogart's, he was too much of a likely lad to have around the place.

Being a Tuesday day shift, only one other person would be at work in Bogart's with The Milky Bar Kid, and myself; female of course. Her name was Stacey, and she hailed from the renowned county of Essex. I was desperate for it to be true, what they said about Essex girls, for Stacey was a truly desirable creature. She had long blonde hair, black roots which for me added to her allure, a pretty face and, most importantly, huge breasts.

Shallow, I admit, but how I wanted to cry my problems into that bosom. Secrets, that I shall take to my grave, would have been spewed forth, had I only had the opportunity to take refuge in that splendid section of paradise.

'Morning Whisky,' she said as she swept into the office.

'Morning Stacey,' I fawned. 'Where'd you go after work last night?' I'd asked her to stay for a drink, but she had declined.

'I went out round to Andrea's, she was having a party.'

'Ah, so you're a bit hung over then?'

'Yeah.'

'Fancy a tipple to take the edge of it?'

'Yeah.'

'Well here's a tenner, go next door and buy a bottle of whatever wine you want.'

'Ah, cheers Whisk, you're the best.'

'Hey, don't mention it,' I said, watching her magnificent posterior as she wiggled it out of the office.

What a woman, I thought, and she was only here until September too, after which she would be returning to college. If I were ever fortunate enough to worm my way into Stacey's pants, the timing of her departure would be perfect. This was because my long-standing girlfriend of two and a half years would be returning to camp in November, albeit only for a weekend. Her name was Rachael and we had met while working at Butlins.

Rachael had taken a job this season working for Club 18-30's as a holiday rep and had been posted to Tenerife, the lucky bitch. We had both applied, but only she had been taken on, and I insisted on her taking the post, rather than rejecting it and maybe regretting it later in life. I have to admit that I also envisaged myself shagging like a whoremonger at a brothel's happy hour, while she was away, but it hadn't quite worked out like that.

Ironically, while Rachael was still working here, it seemed like I was George bloody Clooney. I was constantly propositioned, but dared not do anything in case I was discovered. Now that I was free to act as I wished, I was evidently deemed only slightly more attractive than gonorrhoea and despite my machiavellian scheming I had still only managed to get through a couple holidaymakers. More worrying still, the latter of these two shags had only lasted about five seconds, no doubt due to the infrequency with which I was now using my genitals for purposes other than pissing.

Chapter 3

When I finished work I went straight over to the food and beverage office, where I picked up my mail. There was one letter for me, with Spanish stamps, obviously from Rachael. I tucked it into my pocket and set off back to my chalet.

As I Ambled along Y block, I contemplated Stacey's excuse for not coming to Sweeney's party. She already had plans, she claimed. I wondered if she was lying, not wanting to reject me two nights in a row. After all I was her supervisor, she might find it awkward to work with me afterwards. I fretted as to whether she was telling her friends that her boss was coming on to her, maybe she'd even report me to the management. Nah, I thought, I only asked invited her to a bloody party, thank god I didn't tell her what kind of party it was.

Back at my shed, I threw on some reasonably clean clothes and splashed on some of The Beastmaster's 'shagbait', a curious term he used for his fake aftershaves. I then retired back into my room and opened the letter.

Hiya Whisk,

How's Butlins? I've been really busy this week, worked over seventy hours already and still got one shift left (the big one, changeover day). Last night was pretty cool. We did the final night show, where the reps put on a bit of a stage performance for the guests. We did a rude version of Jack and the Beanstalk (oh you should have seen the beanstalk) and it was a great laugh, though I have to admit it left me feeling a bit randy. God I wish you were here.

Not much else going on really, just work, got to do the airport run tomorrow but Taylor is helping me out so it should be a bit of a laugh. Sorry I haven't written more but

*it's four in the morning and I'm up for work again at nine.
God have mercy on me.*

Love you loads, can't wait to see you again.

All my love,

Rachael xxx

So Taylor was helping her out eh? I just bet he was, the sly
fucker. I seemed to be hearing his name a lot in her letters
recently. Was she trying to make me jealous or something? I
scoured my room for a pen, tore off a few sheets of paper
from my A4 notepad and began to compose my reply. I
made sure to ask her, discreet like, whether this chancer
Taylor had a girlfriend.
When I'd finished writing I placed the letter in an envelope
and left it at the side of the bed to be posted later. I then
jumped up and made my way over to Dale's.
He shared a chalet with a couple of psychotic scousers
called Steve and Charlie. I had deliberately waited until after
six o' clock so that I could be sure they were working. Just
being in the same chalet as those nutters made me uneasy,
but then again so did Dale. I banged on the door and after a
few seconds it opened. Dale stood before me, wearing just a
pair of boxer shorts. He was red faced and sweating so I
deduced that he had either been shagging, wanking or
working out.
'All right mate, come in,' he said.
'Yeah, I ain't staying long, just came to drop of your
money.'
'You not gonna have a joint before you go?'
I didn't like to turn Dale down. Saying no to him was an
exceptionally perilous pursuit.

'Yeah, go on then, just one,' I replied, thinking he was planning to use his own pot.

'Get your gear out then you cunt.'

Typical.

Dale's room was an absolute disgrace, even by Butlins' standards. The floor was covered in Sugar puffs, which I recalled him spilling about three weeks ago. They had been ground into a fine powder after being trodden and re-trodden upon. No wonder this place was infested with rats. His bed sheets were a dirty brown colour rather than the dirty yellow that the rest of us had and an ashtray on the cupboard looked like it hadn't been emptied all season, the place reeked of stale smoke.

I gave him his money then rolled up a small joint, noting his disapproving glare as I rationed out the grass, and lit the thing up.

'What you up to tonight?' he asked.

'Er, I'm meeting Sweeney, just chilling out round at his.'

'Getting stoned?'

'Not really, might have a few beers.'

Please God, don't let this twat invite himself round, Sweeney would go fucking mad.

'I don't think Sweeney likes me, do you?'

He was right, Sweeney hated the cunt.

'What makes you say that?'

'Just the way he looks at me. I can tell when people don't like me you know.'

Was this directed at me? Did he realise that I didn't particularly like him? God, I hoped not.

'I'm not bothered,' he continued. 'I don't particularly like that cunt either. One of these days he might get a fucking smack.'

I sat there for about twenty minutes listening to this dickhead regaling me tales of his numerous fistfights, before politely taking my leave.

'Got to go mate, he's expecting me at seven.'

'I'll follow you out, I'm off for a pint over the Irish bar. Remind me of the old country.'

Old country! This dickhead was about as Irish as Yorkshire pudding, he'd probably never even been to the old country.

'OK mate, I'll see you tomorrow.'

…

Sweeney's pad was the diametric opposite of Dale's. As a supervisor, like me, his chalet had a living room and two bedrooms. But where we had an upturned box, Sweeney had a proper coffee table, he also had a colour television and, luxury of luxuries, a video recorder. The windows had proper curtains, made from thick material, which actually kept light out unlike the standard yellow ones we had that merely altered its shade. Bean bags and Bedouin style cushions lined the walls, and the room was softly lit by various shaded lamps around the room, as opposed to the single naked light bulb that dangled from the ceiling of every other shed on camp. It was, in short like Graceland compared to everyone else's sheds.

Sweeney was able to live in relative opulence, due to a number of reasons. Firstly, he was canny; most of the electrical goods had been procured from members of staff who had brought these items from home when they first arrived. After a few months of Butlins' wages, they became desperate for cash, and would begin selling off valuables. With most other staff in a similar predicament, it was a buyer's market and goods could be obtained cheaply. Secondly, despite his love of 'luxuries' Sweeney was a bit of a tight bastard, he was usually the last to get the rounds in, never really offered his cigarettes out and restricted himself to two nights out a week. Finally, the source of Sweeney's relative wealth was his off-season activities. At the end of each season, and just before each new one, he would book into a clinic for a week and let them test new vaccines and medicines on him. A thousand pounds for a week's work, if you could call it that. When asked if he was worried about any potential complications he would mock us, pointing out the amount of illegal narcotics that we paid to shove down our throats.

There was music inside Sweeney's pad, but unlike the rest of camp it was playing at a sensible level. He was playing Pink Floyd's, *Dark Side of the Moon.*

'All right mate, did you get them?'

'Yes I did,' he replied.

'Nice one, how many each?'

'About seventy.'

'Fuck! Am I the first one here?'

'Yeah, Scary's already off his face in his room.'

'Typical.'

'You know Scary.'

'Beastmaster's not here then?'

'He's gone to get Nicky and Charlotte. How come you're late anyway?'

'I just popped in on Dale.'

'Dale?'

'Yeah, Dale Fortune, from Tipi's.'

'Fucking soldier of fortune! What you doing hanging around with that cock?'

'I'm not hanging around with him. I just paid him a visit after work.'

'Well you better not bring the twat round here. Mark my words mate, that fucker's bad news. If you're around when he gets the sack, he'll no doubt take you down with him. Stay clear son, stay clear.'

I heard a knock at the door and Sweeney went to his room to peer through his curtain.

'It's The Beastmaster, with the girls. What's with that beard anyway?' Sweeney remarked. 'He looks like the bastard son of The Yorkshire Ripper, or General Zod from

Superman Two. By the way, you keep away from Charlotte, the fit one, I'm after her tonight.'

Fair enough, his party.

'WHISKY!!' The Beastmaster greeted me, as though we hadn't seen each other for years, when in fact we actually shared a chalet. I shook his hand and turned to the girls.

'Hi Charlotte, hi...'

'Nicky,' she finished. 'Whisky, is it?'

'Yeah.'

'Interesting name.'

'Well it's not really my name, it just rhymes with it.'

'Frisky?'

'By nature, yes. By name, I'm afraid not.'

She laughed, tossing back her long dark curls. She was a big girl, but not as ugly as Sweeney had made out earlier.

'Well if this is a tea party, where is the tea?'

'Coming right up,' Sweeney interjected. 'Ladies and gentlemen, tea is served.'

In his hands Sweeney held a tray upon which were five cups containing a powerful mushroom tea, Scary having already consumed his. The mushrooms had been hand picked by Scary about a week ago, and he'd been drying out in his room ever since.

'I say,' said The Beastmaster, affecting a posh accent. 'Anyone for high tea.'

Chapter 4

We sat around Sweeney's living room, waiting for the tea to take hold. I positioned myself between Scary and Sweeney while The Beastmaster placed himself strategically between the girls. He was in a state of great excitement and I wondered to myself whether it was the prospect of the mushrooms or a shag that had him in such high spirits. It wasn't as if adding another notch to his heavily scarred bedpost would be anything novel, so I reasoned it must have been the drugs.

I watched him intently as he held court, pontificating to Nicky about various Butlins issues, until eventually they began arguing about his assertion that the Butlins' Redcoat was an outdated concept. She had brought it upon herself by insinuating that they were the main attraction, and the chief reason that customers came here.

'That's bullshit!' he sneered. 'Redcoats are just over hyped baby-sitters.'

'No they're not. They are the focal point of the whole camp. They may be children's entertainers but they're certainly not baby-sitters. Each and every one of them has a talent, in fact you have to have at least one talent in order to get the job.'

'And juggling is a talent is it?' I asked.

'What's juggling got to do with it?' Nicky replied.

'Well,' I elaborated, 'that Michael fellow, who lives in K32, that's his talent. That and riding a uni-cycle. The Beastmaster's right, they're nobodies, like the rest of us. A circus reject here, a mediocre karaoke singer there, that's not talent, that's unfulfilled ambition. It's no different to me, I certainly never intended to work in this shit hole but it's where life has brought me. The same can be said for those guy's, you think they dreamed of being redcoats since they were kids? I don't think so, they dreamed of being pop stars or actors, but weren't good enough. The nearest thing they could get was being a Redcoat, and like The Beastmaster says they're nothing but stuck up child minders.'

'I never said stuck up,' The Beastmaster pointed out.

'Yeah, but they are though aren't they? I passed two of them on my way to work this morning and said hello, but they just fucking blanked me, like I was a piece of shit on their stupid red shoes.'

'Ah, so that's why you don't like them,' Nicky shouted, pointing an accusing finger in my direction. 'You think they look down on you.'

'You're *all* right, ' Sweeney announced, 'in your own little ways. The Beastmaster claims that they are glorified baby-sitters, and he's correct. A large proportion of their job *is* spent trying to baby-sit the horde of screaming brats that infest this camp. But Nicky's right too, they *are* the focal point of the camp. Whenever you tell someone back home that you work at Butlins, what's the first thing they say? 'Are you a redcoat?' You think Butlins, you think redcoats. But, that's not to say that they are the reason people come here. What's the first thing that springs to mind when you think about Disneyland, or Disneyworld? It's Mickey Mouse, but that doesn't mean people travel all the way to Florida to see some half-wit in a Mickey Mouse costume does it? Redcoats are incidental, the fucking half-wits in the costumes. As for what Whisky said about them being stuck up, well he's right, for the most part, they're a bunch of narcissistic tossers, that act like signing a few throwaway autographs for a bunch of eight year old shitheads equals stardom. Well it doesn't.'

We sat and listened to Sweeney's reverence, he pretty much ended that particular debate there and then. The conversation turned to The Beastmaster's new part time occupation on camp. He had started working overtime for the camp's photo shop, wearing various superhero costumes that allowed him to show off his massive appendage while having his photo taken with kids. It was all a bit perverse if you asked me but The Beastmaster was loving it. The Power Ranger costume was his favourite.

'Nice and tight,' he said rubbing his hands together. 'Show the ladies what's on offer.' He turned and winked at Nicky and she giggled and winked back.

I shook my head and wondered to myself how someone with so few standards could be blessed in such a way. The Beastmaster was renowned for his prodigious phallus and, had it not been for his partiality for women that looked like swamp hogs, he would have still been known by his original nickname 'The Gifted One'.

I was still considering this cruel twist of fate when I realised that Scary was having one of his funny turns at the side of me. He'd taken the mushrooms a good two hours before us and had been sitting so quietly, listening to our conversation, that I'd almost forgotten he was there.

For the last couple of minutes however, he had started shifting his weight uncomfortably and scratching at himself as though he were covered in fire ants. I tried not to let him know that I had noticed this, as this would no doubt make him even more self conscious, but unfortunately Nicky had spotted his bizarre behaviour too and was starring at him as though he were a circus freak.

Scary must have noticed her staring, because, without any warning whatsoever he jumped up in his seat and set off running into the bathroom, as though he were about to shit himself. I heard the bath running and knew what this meant. He always sought refuge in cold baths whenever suffering from one of his panic attacks. I had witnessed it on many occasions but Nicky seemed disturbed.

'What's wrong with him?' she asked.

'Nothing to worry about,' Sweeney answered. 'He just suffers with his nerves, especially while on acid or marijuana. He'll be all right again in half an hour.'

'Oh, I was scared that he might be on a bad trip. I was starting to wish I hadn't drunk that bloody tea. You don't think it's gonna have that effect on me do you?'

'Na! That's just how he is. A nervous disposition is all, except when he's on speed or booze. I don't know why he doesn't just stick to booze to tell you the truth. His nerves are fine when he's pissed,' Sweeney reassured her as he stood up to turn off the kitchen light. 'But then again his hangovers make him just as b.. fuck me! Did you see that?'

'What?' I asked.

'Across the wall. From the light switch to the light,' he answered.

'I saw it,' said The Beastmaster.

'What?'

'Electricity. Or something, when Sweeney turned on the switch...'

'...You could see the, electricity...like lightening or something...it went up the wall and across the roof to the lamp,' Sweeney added, his eyes wide with amazement.

'Tea's working then,' I noted, as if it wasn't bloody obvious.

Chapter 5

By the time Scary returned we were almost literally away with the fairies. Sweeney's Bedouin style chalet seemed, to me, to be the most comfortable place in the world and I melted into his huge cushions, while I let the music wrap itself around me.

The tunes, as always in Sweeney's shed, were psychedelic. And the conversation revolved around the unusual hallucinations that the party were experiencing. For whatever reason, I could not see any of the mad shit that everyone else was describing and suspected that they were making a lot of it up.

I was however having trouble looking in the direction of an increasingly demonic looking Beastmaster, whose freshly grown facial hair *did* give him an uncanny resemblance to General Zod, from *Superman Two*.

'Come to me son of Jerel! Kneel before Zod!' I shouted, almost involuntarily.

'What?' asked The Beastmaster.

'Take my hand and swear eternal loyalty…to Zod,' Sweeney added.

'What the fuck are you talking about?' he asked defensively as we rolled round pissing ourselves.

'Nothing general,' I said, chuckling and closing my eyes to take refuge in the music.

Tune after tune came, each one more bizarre than the last, and with them an array of images and visions swirled in and out of my head.

Around me I was aware of the others but preferred to enjoy my own private trip. I occasionally opened an eye, just to accept a cigarette or joint but for the most part ignored everyone else and swam in my own mind. A few hours later, I realised that doors were being opened and closed and that there were fewer voices in the room. Then the stereo became quieter and I opened an eye to check that we weren't being kicked out. We weren't. Sweeney was leading Charlotte towards his bedroom, but The Beastmaster and Nicky were still giggling quietly on the couch. Scary was nowhere to be seen, no doubt he was either having one of his funny turns or was out trying to pick some more mushrooms.

I closed my eyes again and drifted into the next song, Jefferson Airline's *White Rabbit.*

> *One pill makes you larger*
> *And one pill makes you small.*
> *And the ones that mother gives you*
> *Don't do anything at all.*
> *Go ask Alice*
> *When she's ten feet tall.*

Opening an eye, I attempted to focus. Across the room I could see The Beastmaster sitting back in the couch, starring straight at me, a huge grin on his face. His stomach seemed to be bursting open, like *Alien* or *The Thing* was about to pop out. I starred at it in horror as I realised that something was. It was a face coming out of his stomach. I blinked and concentrated, his smile was immense, did he not realise what was happening to him? I wanted to shout at him, warn him what was happening. Then, suddenly, reality came back into focus. The head wasn't coming out of his stomach at all. It was bobbing up and down on his massive member. No wonder the cunt was smiling.

He motioned me over with his head, while I struggled to focus properly on what was happening.

'You don't mind if Whisky joins us, do you?' he hissed at Nicky.

She looked unsure, before eventually replying: 'Come over here then, get your dick out. Let's see if it's as big as this fucker.'

'Not likely,' The Beastmaster scoffed.

I dragged myself up and made my way confusedly over to them. The Beastmaster was groping her breasts while she struggled to fit a quarter of his cock into her mouth. I sat next to him and took out my dick. It was flaccid and looked like a child's next to that fucker's huge hard on.

'Told you it wasn't anything like mine,' he laughed.

'Come here,' Nicky encouraged me, though her face looked disappointed. 'Let's get some life into this thing.'

She took my pliant dick in her mouth and began licking the end, slowly rousing me as she did so. The Beastmaster moved behind Nicky and pulled up her dress, before removing her pants. She shifted her weight from knee to knee helping him negotiate them from her legs. With a quick wink in my direction and the flash of his smile, he disappeared beneath her dress and Nicky began to whimper softly while she sucked me off.

> *When the men on the chessboard*
> *Get up and tell you where to go.*
> *And you've just had some kind of mushroom*
> *And your mind is moving low.*
> *Go ask Alice*
> *I think she'll know.*

'Get on the couch,' The Beastmaster ordered her. She got up and pulled off the dress, revealing two plump tits a barrel like stomach and a matt of long hair that looked like it had been pulled out of Michael Bolton's bath plug.

Laying with her back on the couch she spread her legs wide open and began rubbing her flabby breasts. The Beastmaster threw his head into her muff like a donkey attacking a bag of

28

oats. I kissed her half heatedly and she returned it so enthusiastically I had to pull away, deciding instead to return my dick to her mouth.

'Is one of you gonna fuck me then?' she mumbled.

'Oh, we're both gonna fuck you love, don't you worry,' The Beastmaster replied, before turning to me and taking a look at my dick. 'You better go first Whisk.'

We exchanged places and I guided myself into her, without any thoughts of using a condom.

'Hmm,' she groaned as I pushed myself inside. 'I hope you're as good a shag as I think you're going to be.'

I don't know how good she thought I was going to be, but she was wrong. I shot myself into her in a matter of seconds, before apologising and pulling out.

'Step aside, quick draw McGraw,' The Beastmaster commanded. 'I'll take over from here.'

He stood at the side of her with that huge thing held at the base in both his hands, like an executioner about to bring the axe down on her.

'Come on then,' she taunted. 'Let's show him how it's done.'

She opened her legs, wide, and he squeezed himself into her, forcing her to wince as he did so.

'Fuck me, that is big,' she squealed, closing her eyes and screwing her face up as he started to thrust away.'

I sat there watching as he fucked her every which way but loose. Where I had lasted about the length of the chorus in *White Rabbit*, this bastard kept going for the rest of the album.

She squealed in delight, taunting me as to why I couldn't fuck like this animal, while he delighted in giving me instruction as he performed his master class. I did eventually get another hard on but had to contend myself with being wanked off by her, while The Beastmaster shagged her from behind, slapping her arse and winking at me as he did so. I didn't want to risk putting it in her mouth with the fucking he was giving her; she was liable to bite it off.

Eventually, quite a while after she had come, The Beastmaster withdrew and shot himself over her back, rubbing it in afterwards.

'Best fucking moisturiser you can get love,' he told her.

'Fucking hell!' she cried out. 'This boy has got fucking talent!'

They spent the next ten minutes necking on the couch and completely ignoring my presence, so I decided to make myself scarce. I didn't fancy being around when he managed to re-awaken the Kraken and give her another good seeing to. They didn't even look up as I exited the door.

Chapter 6

It was a long night, that one. With no hope of sleep and the prospect of being mocked by both The Beastmaster and Nicky the next day, I worked myself into quite a state. Why had I joined in? I should have known that no good would come from going two's up with that over developed freak. Now I would have to endure all manner of taunts regarding my prowess in the bedroom, and I couldn't even tell him he was talking shit, because I really had been that bad.

That was the problem with issues like this on camp, these things got around, people talked, there was no anonymity. Where in the real world you would be unlikely to see a one night stand again, here you were forced to see them every single bloody day. Now whenever I saw her laughing with a friend in the staff canteen, or the staff bar, I would wonder if she were relaying the tale of my woeful performance.

What was I thinking anyway? I had a girlfriend. Why did I chase other women all the time, when I was so besotted with Rachael? Perhaps it was because she wasn't here and while everyone around you is fucking like they're in a brothel it's hard not to feel left out.

I wished Rachael were there. I wished she hadn't taken that job as a Club 18-30's holiday rep. I knew what those fuckers got up to, that's why I had applied for the job myself. That's why I insisted that if one of us got the job without the other, they had to take it, dickhead that I was, I really believed I was more likely to get the job. Yeah, great plan Bamber fucking Gascoigne, that's why you're sat here now in this fucking three by two shed and she's out there getting off her tits in some club in Tenerife.

I spent the rest of the night worrying about what The Beastmaster and Nicky would say about me. Would they just laugh at my premature ejaculation, or also at my relative size to his? After all, compared to The Beastmaster I was hung like a pre-pubescent Stuart Little, but who wasn't? Would they take that into consideration? Also, what sort of performance did they expect? The Beastmaster might be out fucking every night, but I hadn't had a shag for ages.

But the biggest worry of all, now that my lust had been satisfied was the fear of being caught. Rachael might get to hear about my indiscretion when she returned for the 18-30's reunion party held here in November. To think that twenty seconds of pleasure might jeopardise a three-year relationship. Oh god, what had I done?

All thoughts of sleep were relinquished at about five in the morning after which time I chain smoked about ten Mayfairs in an hour waiting for the canteen to open.

At half past six I skulked over there, frightening a rat that was rummaging in the bags of refuse, dumped at the end of the chalet block, as I passed. I thought about how repulsed I had been when I first saw a rat in my chalet. I hadn't wanted to stay there, I wanted to move sheds, but what would be the point? They were everywhere, the camp was infested with the bloody things. Eventually I had gotten used to them.

Rats didn't bother me now, my only fear was that Nicky and The Beastmaster might be over at the canteen too, but I reasoned that they were probably still shagging. I needn't have worried; I was the only one in there, besides the staff. That was the first breakfast that I had been up in time for this season. Not that I ate any of it, I just wanted the coffee, to try and bring me round a little.

Several cups of shitty freeze dried coffee later I left the canteen and picked up a copy of *The Sun* from Everydays and returned to the shed to read it and wank off over Jenny, twenty-one from Newcastle, the page three girl. The wank took a lot longer than reading the newspaper did and I cursed the irony in the fact that it took me so long to pleasure myself while Nicky had chewed me up and spat me out within a minute.

At ten o' clock I readied myself for work and left the chalet. The Beastmaster hadn't come back yet, which was bad, because it meant that he was still at Scary and Sweeney's pad. This brought about the distinct possibility of him blabbing something to them about last night before I had the opportunity to take him aside and beg him to keep his trap shut.

After checking the safe to make sure nobody else had been plundering it besides me, I put a float into the till and prepared one for the hot dog bike. I then retired to the office, closing the door to let it be known to Stacey and Andy that I was not to be disturbed. Fortunately there were no windows in the office and I switched off the lights, and sat there in the dark, trying to rest my eyes.

Around mid-day the telephone rang and woke me up, I picked it up and mumbled sleepily into the mouthpiece, 'Bogart's. Paul Hisky speaking.'

'Hello Paul, it's Lorraine. Could you come over to the management office, we are having a meeting and need you here.'

'A meeting? What kind of meeting?'

'Never mind that now, just come on over and I will fill you in when you get here.'

A meeting. What the hell was all this about? We only ever had meetings when someone was being fired, or promoted. Was I being promoted? I seriously doubted it, so I must be being fired. Yes that was it, I was getting the boot. They'd somehow got wind of my fiddling, maybe Dale had been caught and implicated me, to prevent them taking police action against him.

Grassing bastard.

'I'm nipping over to the office for a while,' I shouted to Stacy as I swept through the kitchen towards the fire door.

'If you need any change, you'll have to get it from
Everydays next door.'

I lit up a Mayfair, for the sake of my nerves, and hurried
my way over to the other side of camp. Normally I would
cover up my uniform, as it was frowned upon to smoke in it,
but as I was probably getting the sack anyway I didn't
bother. At the entrance to the management office I
extinguished the butt on the wall and regarded my shaking
hands, which were dripping with sweat. I wiped them on my
trousers, took a deep breath and entered the office.

'Hi Paul,' said Julie, Lorraine's secretary. 'They're waiting
for you in there.'

'Cheers Julie,' I croaked, wondering who the fuck *they*
were.

I gave the door a cursory knock, before shoving it open.
Inside, Lorraine, the stumpy little customer catering
manager, with her ridiculous Kevin Keegan style perm and
owl like spectacles, was sat at the end of the table looking
sternly in my direction. Around the table sat a dozen or so
worried looking section leaders and team leaders from the
department.

'Hi Paul, take a seat,' Lorraine ordered, motioning me to a
chair opposite her. 'Sorry to drag you all from your venues
like this but I felt I needed to speak to every supervisor with
their own venue in the department. As you all know, we
have a full audit four times a season in addition to your
weekly stock take. Unfortunately we have found several
disturbing discrepancies in our latest audit. In a number of
venues, stock is several thousand pounds down. Now, I
know that wastage and over portioning can be an issue, but
we are talking thousands of pounds here ladies and
gentlemen. I have ordered a re-audit, just in case the figures
are incorrect, but I seriously doubt that.'

Shit! I almost jumped out of my chair at this, literally. A
re-audit! One audit was bad enough, but a re-audit would

show the extent of the pillaging we had been up to in the intervening weeks. I always slowed down on the embezzlement before an audit, and made sure I transferred stock from one venue to another (off the books of course) to cover my tracks. The re-audit may well expose how grossly inaccurate the figures were at the original one.

'Which venues were down?' enquired Sian, a team leader from the fish and chip shop at The Showboat.

'Every single venue in the department was down, but some were down more than others.'

'When is this re-audit?' I chipped in, desperate for information so that I might start planning how to cover up my misappropriation.

'Probably today or tomorrow,' she answered, staring at me suspiciously. I was sure she knew why I asked this, and could feel myself turning paler as her eyes bore into me.

Barely Breathing Brian, the antediluvian shift leader from The Gaiety, who after twenty odd years of service was starting to resemble Albert Steptoe jumped up, almost spitting his false teeth out as he did so.

'The Gaiety Theatre can't have been down,' he declared. 'I'm no thief.'

No but I am you old fucker! A re-audit today or tomorrow! How could I move stock in that time?

'Brian, nobody is being accused of being a thief,' Lorraine answered him, while seemingly staring at me. 'As I have already stated, wastage and over portioning can be attributed to part of this discrepancy. However, in a couple of venues the shortfall cannot be so easily accounted for. That is not to say that anyone here is a thief, I am merely stating that stock is going missing. This could be due to a number of reasons, and we need to look at the way we are operating. First of all, I am going to need all of you to keep wastage sheets, detailing every single item that has to be discarded. Secondly we need to keep an eye on staff. I want staff that are over portioning disciplined and staff that are under-ringing sent to me. Thirdly we need to look at the security of stock, I want all stock to be put away the minute it arrives at the venue, this is best practice anyway for health and safety as well as hygiene reasons. Then we need to ensure that the stock rooms are locked whenever they are unsupervised. If staff *are* stealing from the stockroom, these measures should help stamp it out. Is everybody clear on this?'

'Yes,' we chorused. I personally only just managed to croak the word out. My mouth had become completely devoid of moisture, either through panic, fear or the comedown. I was moving uncomfortably on my seat and drawing strange looks from the other occupants of the room, including Lorraine, who seemed to direct everything she said at me. Look at someone else you tubby bitch! I wanted to shout.

Lorraine then went on to outline what measures she would be taking to improve security in those venues that did not have a lockable stock room and assure us all that if we followed her guidelines that we needn't worry about future discrepancies. When she eventually finished she asked if we had any questions, to which Barely Breathing Brian asked about twenty. Fuck me, hadn't the old bastard been here long enough to know correct portion sizes, I thought. After almost three decades in the job he should know these things inside out.

No one else asked any questions, least of all me. I just needed to get out of this room. My movements were becoming erratic, like I had Parkinson's disease. My hands were pouring out sweat at an alarming rate and I was sure, absolutely certain, that all colour had drained from my face.

'Right then, if no-one has any questions, I shall let you all return to your venues. Please implement these new measures with immediate effect, I don't want another audit as bad as this one.'

We all stood and began filing out of the office. Being near the back of the room, I would have to wait for the others to get out first, but I was desperate for fresh air. I was displaying many of the symptoms that I had seen in Scary, while he was having one of his panic attacks and realised that if I didn't calm myself down quickly I would probably have one myself. Fresh air, that's what would sort me out, fresh air and a glass of water. I needed out of this office and I needed out now.

'Excuse me,' I said as I barged past Sian, from The Showboat. Another apology was made to Barely Breathing Brian as I bumped past him; I wanted to shout at them all, get out my fucking way! Could they not see I was ill, I needed fresh air, damn them.

'Paul,' Lorraine called.

'Yes,' I answered, still pushing my way out.

'Could you hold back a moment? I'd like a word.'

You...greasy fucking lard mountain.

'Er, sure. Can I call over later, I need the toilet really quite badly?'

'One minute won't hurt.'

It bloody will. I'm freaking out here.

'OK,' I replied, twitching enviously as the others departed. When the last of them left, I watched my escape hatch closing behind them.

'Are you all right Paul?' she asked, more out of duty than concern.

'Yeah, yeah I just need the toilet, really badly.'

'Ok Paul, I'll make it quick then. Your venue was particularly poor in the audit. The guidelines that I have set out are going to apply to you most of all. I have also decided that Bogart's is perhaps a little too large a venue for just one section leader, I am therefore moving Richard Honeyman over from Mr. B's. You will still be in charge of shift rotas and running the shifts that you work, while Richard will run all other shifts as well as having responsibility for stock take. Is this clear?'

'Yes. Is that all?'

'For now, yes. Richard will move to Bogart's with immediate effect, I have already informed him and he will commence duty this evening. I want you to co-operate with him and I am sure the two of you will make a great success of Bogart's in future. Ok, you'd better go quickly, you don't look very well.'

My hand slid off the door handle as I tried to fumble it open. I dried it against my trousers and made another, more successful attempt. Outside I tried to regain my composure but could feel my breathing becoming more shallow and rapid, I was hyperventilating. That bitch was onto me, and Richard's arrival would no doubt herald my downfall. But right now I couldn't give a flying toss, I just wanted this anxiety attack to piss off. A surge of electricity shot down my left arm, numbing my fingers and giving me the impression I was having a heart attack.

Panic stations.

What did Scary do in this situation? The bath. Run for it. Your salvation lies in the bath.

Chapter 7

My hands were shaking like a Geiger counter needle at Chernobyl and my legs were seemingly made out of wine gums. A strange and terrifying feeling washed over me, if I didn't get into that bath I was going to die. My heart rate was accelerating to an alarming rate, we were in heart attack territory here, real serious shit. My back was itching like a prostitute's privates and my clammy palms struggled to grip the taps. As I disrobed I noticed that my genitals had shrivelled to microscopic proportions, and to cap it all off I couldn't muster up enough saliva to swallow. It's amazing how desperate you become to swallow, when you cannot perform the fucking action, real desperate, as though struggling for air.

Panic stations were fully manned, the symptoms were all present, here it came again. Aggghhrr, the jolt burst down my left arm like an electric shock, terrifying and numbing at the same time. Get in the bath, get in the fucking bath. It was still only about an inch deep, but I needed that bath like a diabetic needs insulin. I dived in and felt a degree of instant relief as the coldness of the water hit me.

About thirty minutes later I began to shake uncontrollably again. This time however I knew it was because my body temperature was dropping, rather than another anxiety attack. The thought of leaving my icy sanctuary filled me with dread, but I had to leave it or I risked hypothermia. I got out and towelled myself off, noting how damp and musty the towel smelled.

Ten minutes later I realised my hands were drenched again, a tell tale sign of what was in the post. I suddenly became aware of my own heartbeat, dum ...dum, dum..dum, dum.dum, dumdum, it seemed to be racing. Fuck! Shit! Here we go again and this time I couldn't get in the bath, I still hadn't warmed back up yet. It had to be the booze, that was

Scary's other method, he washed away the panic with alcohol.

I ran as though I were pursued by furies, straight for Everydays. Picking up a bottle of Thunderbirds (black label) that most ignoble of fortified wines I headed, twitchily towards the counter.

'Four pounds please,' the checkout girl informed me.

'Keep the change,' I said, depositing a fiver in her hand.

I exited the shop and, with trembling hands, attempted to remove the bottle top. No use, my hands were too wet, I dried them against my thighs and attempted once more. A wave of euphoria and relief washed over me as the top came loose, and I drank greedily from the bottle on the steps outside. Instant relief. The booze transformed the needles in my brain into the fingers of a master masseuse. Here was the answer, low-grade alcohol.

It suddenly occurred to me that I was chugging Thunderbirds, from the bottle, pretty much outside my place of work, while in uniform. Christ, in my panic I had completely forgotten that I was supposed to be working. I put the bottle inside my blue jacket and wiped the residue from my lips, while taking a quick look around to make sure that no management were in the area.

I opened the fire exit to Bogart's and made my way through the kitchen.

'Hiya Whisk,' Stacey greeted me. 'Thought you weren't coming back.'

'Yeah, sorry I was so long. Lorraine hasn't called in the last half hour or so has she?'

'No, no-one's called at all.'

'Good, good. I'm going to be in the office for a while, when it gets quiet you can grab us a bottle of Taboo, if you like.'

'Sounds great, a bottle of Taboo it is.'

'Actually, better make it two bottles,'

Chapter 8

By the end of the shift, Stacey and I were both quite pissed. We giggled childishly and made jokes at the milky bar kid's expense. The sweet, sweet wine had washed all thoughts of the horrible experience I'd endured earlier away. Stacey wasn't quite as drunk as I was but she was becoming increasingly tactile; grabbing my arm each time I cracked a joke. I could very well be in here, I mused.

We had to tone it down a little when we saw Richard coming through the tunnel towards us. It wouldn't do to have that bastard snitching to Lorraine on his first day. I'd had the foresight to tell Stacey to buy a packet of extra strong mints while getting in the Taboo and we had been sucking on them a good ten minutes when Dickie arrived on the scene.

'Hi Paul,' he hailed me, as he entered the kitchen.

'Please, call me Whisky.'

'OK Whisky, do you want to show me where everything is?'

'Er, not at the moment Richie, old boy. I'm really hungry and need to get over to the staff canteen ASAP.'

'Well you don't finish for another ten minutes.'

So it was like that was it Richie, old boy? OK I'll show you round you twat.

'Fair enough mate, follow me and I'll give you the grand tour.'

The grand tour lasted exactly ten minutes. Richard wanted to know more but I informed him that if he needed to know where anything was, the night staff should be able to help him out. I took my leave at exactly five thirty and ignoring Andy completely, I turned to Stacey and suggested dinner at the staff canteen.

'Yeah Whisk, sounds good. Can I meet you over there? I'd rather get out of this bloody uniform first if you don't mind.'

'Sure, I'll see you over there.'

Getting changed eh? Maybe she was keen after all. If she turned up in her Sunday best, I was in for sure. I almost skipped my way to the other side of camp. What had started out as a disastrous day was quickly turning into a potential beauty.

Being after five thirty, when many people were on their night shifts, the staff canteen was pretty empty. A few catering staff here, a security guard there, just the guys who worked day shifts or those that started really late. I approached the counter and observed the delights on offer. It was basically the same shit that they served at breakfast. No doubt the lack of patrons that morning had meant they had plenty of stuff to re heat and get rid of. Still I was a lot hungrier than I had been that morning and I ordered sausage egg and chips from Long John Silver behind the counter.

'Any beans or hash browns?' he asked, grinning inanely.

'No mate, those hash browns leave a coat on my teeth that only a bloody blow torch could remove,' I slurred in reply.

No answer, just the grin.

I took my meal and headed for an empty table near the entrance, where Stacey would come in. Shit, I thought as I placed down my food, I forgot to get some toast. Staggering back to the counter I picked up a couple of toasted slices of brown bread; I always stuck to brown after a lengthy battle with constipation and piles in the previous season. The toast was cold, which I fully expected it to be, but it was still reasonably pliable, and therefore edible. I returned to the plate of sausage, egg and chips over by the entrance and began drunkenly gorging on my meal.

'Oi, what the fuck do you think you're doing?' came an angry voice behind me. 'You're eating my bloody dinner.'

'Er, I think you'll find this is my dinner,' I replied, turning around to face a mean looking, shaven headed security guard, known around camp as Knuckles.

'No it's not. I put that meal there just thirty seconds ago, while I went to grab a coffee. Now you're eating my food, you prick.'

'Who the fuck are you calling a prick?' I demanded, foolishly standing up. Knuckles was a good six inches taller than me and infinitely bigger in build.

'I'm calling you a prick, you skinny little twat. Now I'll ask you again, why are you eating my fucking dinner?'

'I've told you, I'm not eating your…' looking down two tables, I could clearly see my dinner of, sausage egg and chips sitting exactly where I had put it. Shit, in my drunkenness, I had evidently sat back at the wrong table and started eating this beast's dinner. Still, no matter, this was easily resolved, he could simply have mine.

'Oh shit, sorry mate. You're right, I'm so stupid. I can see my dinner just there. I must have sat back at the wrong table by accident. Sorry.'

'Yeah well sorry's not gonna get my dinner back is it?'

'Calm down pal. It's not like you can't get another, you can have mine, or get a fresh one from the counter. It is free remember.'

'Maybe to you dickhead, but I don't live on camp. I have to pay for mine.'

'Don't worry pal, have mine.'

'I don't fucking want yours, and I'm not your pal, fuckwit.'

'I tell, you what mate, stick your fucking dinner up your arse,' I snapped pointing at him with the butter knife I'd been using on my toast.

In an instant the knife was knocked from my hand and I was on the floor with my arm up my back. He was so strong I could do nothing except grab his testicles with my free hand, I twisted and squeezed as hard as I could and heard him scream as I did so. This move seemed to anger Knuckles just as much as it hurt him and my arm went further up my back and his knee dug into my ribs as another hand clasped itself around my throat, cutting off my air supply. I let go of his testicles, reasoning that he might let me breathe if I did so, but I was wrong, I choked and gasped for air until another security guard joined the melee.

'What's up?' he asked.

'This fucker pulled a knife on me,' Knuckles informed him.

'It was a bloody butter knife, for god's sake,' I choked.

They dragged me up from the floor and led me, gagging violently out of the canteen. As we exited I noticed Stacey coming from the direction of the staff quarters, she was all done up, I'd have been in there, I noted as they dragged me to the security office.

Chapter 9

Des Bailey was the security manager for Butlins, Skegness. Tall, skinny, and with a moustache and side parting that make him look not dissimilar to Adolph Hitler he was every inch the failed copper.

Des, or D to his friends was, for want of a more poetic turn of phrase, full of shit. Capable of weaving tales, more fantastical than any comic book writer, he would have you believe that he was Superman, Batman and The Fantastic Four all rolled into one. Able to leap cardboard chalets in a single bound, the only thing standing between a camp-wide crime epidemic and us was the agility and fortitude of Des Bailey.

The premise of Desmond's legendary adventures invariably began with a variation of the same well-worn line: 'There were these (insert any number higher than three here) of them, right.'

The yarns would then end in a similarly predictable manner, i.e. with the bunch of blokes (all of whom were massive, of course) rolling around on the floor, ruing the day that they had tangled with Des Bailey.

Only a naive schoolboy would actually believe any of his bullshit stories, but he himself seemed oblivious to his reputation as a shit-slinger, and I am sure he had told the stories so many times that he himself, now believed them to be true.

Still, Des did have a saving grace, as far as I was concerned anyway and that was that he seemed to like me. I knew that my being sacked was not a foregone conclusion, as long as Des Bailey was in charge of my disciplinary hearing. He had not been on duty the previous evening, when I was unceremoniously dragged into the security office, which was a real bonus. If he had been, he would have noted that I was steaming drunk and that I had just finished work, I might

possibly have been sacked. As it was I had merely been
confined to my chalet, and told to report to Des the
following morning for a disciplinary hearing.

Sweeney had gotten word, via The Beastmaster, of my
predicament and had called round to give me some
invaluable advice.

'The trick with Des,' he'd told me, 'is to get him telling
you one of his war stories. He loves anyone who indulges
his tales of derring-do.'

I entered the security office and looked around. There were
various clippings from the local press regarding the exploits
of Butlins' security staff from years gone by. One clip told
of a stash of ecstasy that had been uncovered by the police,
with the help of the camp's security staff during last year's
18-30's reunion. I remembered the bust, it had meant that
we'd been forced to make do with speed for the entire
weekend. What with work, whiz and wanking that weekend
I hadn't slept for over seventy two hours, a personal record.

'Paul!' I heard Des shout me from inside his office. I got
up and entered.

'Morning Des, morning Matt.'

'Morning,' replied Des. Knuckles just stared aggressively.
'Sit yourself down Paul.'

'Cheers.'

'Now, Matt here has told me his side of the story,
apparently you threatened him with a knife, is that right?'

'I wouldn't say that I threatened him, I merely pointed it at
him.'

'Yeah, in a threatening manner,' cried Knuckles.

'Matt, it was a butter knife, was I threatening to butter you
to death?'

'You waved the knife in my face, which is why I had to
take you down.'

'Take me down? Fucking hell Matt, you're not Eliot Ness.'

'I'll have no swearing in here,' Interrupted Des.

'Sorry Des. Look, it was all a big misunderstanding. I sat down with my dinner, sausage, egg and chips, I went back to the counter and sat back down to what I thought was my dinner. That's when Matt comes in, guns blazing, like I'm trying to nick his food. Why would I nick his dinner, it's free, it was all a mistake, admittedly on my part, but Matty here wouldn't accept my apology.'

'Yes well, Matt says you were drunk, and waving the knife in his face.'

'Des, I had just finished work, how could I be drunk? As for waving the knife in his face, I've told you it was a butter knife, if he's so frightened by a butter knife I think he's in the wrong job. I bet you've been threatened with worse than that in your time haven't you Des?'

'Well actually I was once threatened by these three blokes, one of which was carrying a bloody great chainsaw...'

Bingo.

Chapter 10

I finished work that evening at five thirty on the dot. I thought about asking Stacey out for a drink, but remembered that I was supposed to be meeting Sweeney at Jo Maine's place. Jo was a butch looking girl with short bleached blonde hair and tattoos down her forearms, who lived in a caravan park that could be reached with a stone thrown from Butlins. Our camp was also her livelihood, but not in the conventional way. She made her money by peddling the tsunami of narcotics that washed over camp.

She'd had her door busted down a number of times but all the police had ever found was a thick cloud of smoke and an ice cool female pusher, denying everything.

The police hadn't bothered Jo now for several months and this made her nervous. She was convinced that this meant they were following her covertly in order to find her dealers. I knocked on the caravan door and Jo answered, Sweeney was already sitting in the tiny living room.

'Hi guys,' I said, as Jo let me in.

'Hi Whisk,' replied Jo. 'Sweeney tells me you had a close shave.'

'Yeah, could have been serious that. Good job I've got the grand master advising me eh?'

'They'll never get you while you're with me mate, that's for sure,' Sweeney said tapping his temple.

'You looking forward to the end of the season?' Jo asked me.

'Yeah, can't wait to see Rachael again. I've really been missing her the last few days.'

'You weren't missing her the other night from what I heard,' Sweeney exclaimed.

The Beastmaster. That bastard had blabbed.

'Yeah, well, I'm no angel. What you doing for the 18-30's weekend?' I asked Jo, attempting to change the subject.

'Nothing, I think I'm gonna piss off to Goa for the winter. I've been saving all season and don't want the hassle of being busted every day during weekend breaks. You know how they always crack down when the 18-30's reunion comes to town. It's not worth the risk, I'll spend the winter smoking skunk on an Indian beach rather than freezing in this bloody caravan. Nobody can afford anything round here in the closed season anyway.'

'You can bring some shit with you when you come back.'

'Maybe, but smuggling from places like that is a dodgy business, I think I'll stick to selling on camp.'

'Sounds sensible. What's the plan for tonight then?'

'We're probably gonna go for a few drinks in town.'

'Is there a bus due?' I asked.

'Fuck off! Bus!' Sweeney shouted.

Sweeney hated the bus; he called it the poverty wagon. I should have known better than to ask really, he taxied everywhere.

'No we just called a taxi,' said Jo.

'OK I'll come.'

We sat down and Sweeney pulled out a huge bag of weed and began to roll.

'Just have a cheeky bifta first eh?' he said.

I heard a car outside and sat up.

'Taxi must be here.'

'We didn't order it until seven,' Jo said jumping up and peering round the curtains. 'Shit, Sweeney, flush your gear. Whisky, you got anything?'

'No,' I replied.

I heard the sound of the doors opening, then being shut and then there was an almighty banging on the door.

Sweeney was in the toilet in a second and we heard the flush. Jo answered the door and four officers entered.

'We have a warrant to search the premises,' said one.

'Not again,' said Jo, 'I was just on my way out.'

I heard another flush come from the toilet, but it sounded weak, as though the cistern hadn't been full. One of the policemen banged on the toilet door. Another flush.

'Won't be a minute,' Sweeney called out.

'Open up sir,' shouted the policeman.

Another, very weak, flush.

The policeman pushed the flimsy door, hard. It opened and revealed Sweeney with his hands in the toilet bowl.

'What we got here then?' he asked.

Sweeney had no answer. They searched the rest of the caravan and found nothing. Jo denied all knowledge of whatever Sweeney was trying to flush. He, terrified of her contacts, admitted she had nothing to do with his bag of narcotics. But it was the bankroll that Sweeney always carried that interested the police the most. They knew Jo was dealing, but had no proof. With Sweeney's considerable wad of cash and his ample sized bag of weed they were convinced they had found Jo's dealer.

Chapter 11

The outlanders. The most pitiful of all Skegness residents.
No doubt all the Butlins' towns have outlanders. They live
in a terrible limbo, trapped in the purgatory between Butlins
and the outside world, like Patrick Swayze in *Ghost*, unable
to move on into the next life. Certain satellite companies
such as Fantasy Island were staffed almost entirely by these
wretched creatures. Sacked members of staff from Butlins,
who would do anything to avoid returning to Mansfield,
Dudley, Grantham or whatever shithole it was that they had
arrived from.

I was fairly sure that Sweeney would not go down the route
of the outlander, he had poured scorn on them enough times.
But then, he had been on camp for six years. Like me, he
had lost touch with most of his friends from back home, and
minus his wad, had no provision for life on the outside.

I could feel myself distancing myself from him already, as
though he had some dreadful disease and I feared
contracting it. That's the way it was here, and I knew that
some day my mates would treat me in the same manner. Of
course, I would go through the motions, as I had done many
times before. I would wait for him to return from the
security office, ask how it went, act shocked and upset when
he told me, and help him carry his possessions to the gates
accompanied by the obligatory security guard. We would
say our farewells, promise to keep in touch along with a few
other well-wishers, then he would be forgotten. Sure, maybe
we would tell an amusing anecdote that included him in it,
but after a while, as the inevitable staff turnover took its toll,
our audience would simply ask: 'Who's Sweeney?' and we
would reply casually, 'Oh, just some guy who used to work
here'.

I went back to the window and looked across to Y row.
Still no sign. Huh, he was either giving a Perry Mason style

performance to Des, in a desperate attempt to save his job or
he was encouraging a tale or two from him. Guiltily, I began
thinking of excuses in case he wanted to go for a farewell
drink, *sorry mate, no cash.* Nah, no good, he might offer to
buy. *Can't Sweeney, got work soon.* When had that stopped
me? Then I saw him, accompanied by fucking Knuckles,
who, cock that he was, was wearing a huge grin on his face.

'Sweeney,' I shouted. He looked across, with a sad smile,
confirming what I already knew. 'How did it go?'

'I've got 20 minutes mate, can't talk, gotta get my stuff
together.'

'Want a hand?'

'Yeah, that would be a help.'

I closed my door and made my way over to his shed, trying
my best to look as dejected as he did.

'You gonna stay in Skegness?'

'Don't make me laugh.'

'Not even for tonight?'

'Whisky. Stop talking shit.'

I should have known, Sweeney had far more dignity than
that. No doubt he would love to stay in Skegness, but he had
berated enough others for this crime against nobility that this
would have been an impossible option for him.

'What you doing with the television in your bedroom?' I
asked, immediately cursing myself for such a callous
question.

'It's yours for twenty quid,' he replied.

'I'm not sure I can afford twenty quid mate.'

'Just take it dickhead, it's not like I'm gonna carry it on the
train.'

That's the thing about sackings. They are like the death of
a distant relative, insofar as everyone is a little upset but also
hoping they will be left something in the will. In this case I
had now been upgraded from portable black and white to
colour TV.

'What about the Sega Mega Drive?'

'Don't push it. You cheeky bastard.'

When we had packed his stuff together, we made our way off camp. Sweeney didn't want to take the long ignoble route to the main entrance, where most sackings waited for the bus to take them into town. Instead he opted to leave via the relative quiet of the side entrance from where he would take a taxi. Even now, with his wad in a police evidence bag, and only a week's wage to his name he refused to utilise the services of the poverty wagon. As we trudged along I asked if he had written down his home address, so that me or the lads could write to him.

'No mate, I'll write to you when I get settled,' he said, smiling, knowingly. As we reached the gate, the taxi was waiting, which I think came as a great relief to us both. Better to get this over and done with. A bit like dumping a lover.

'Well it's been a pleasure,' I said extending my hand.

'The pleasure's all yours,' he said jokingly as he shook my hand hard, as though I were somehow responsible for his sacking. I knew he was hurting, he knew I knew it too, but he was damned if he'd say so. He let go of my hand, turned and got in his taxi, and he never looked back. Not while I was in sight anyway.

Chapter 12

It was ironic, Sweeney getting the sack so soon after giving me the advice on how not to. But that was Des, he despised anything to do with drugs. He saw himself as some sort of drugs tsar, and if the police had mentioned my presence at the chalet, he may well have it in for me now too. I thought about this as I picked up my mail, better keep my head down for a while.

There was one letter, postmarked Playa Las Americas. I took it from the pigeonhole, strolled over to the staff canteen and read it over a cup of coffee.

Hiya Whisk,

So Sweeney's still having his tea parties and Scary's still battling his 'old foe' eh? Nothing changes on Butlins. How's The Beastmaster? You didn't mention him in your last letter. I'm sure he hasn't quit, don't tell me he's been sacked.

How come you are so interested in whether Taylor has a girlfriend? Not jealous I hope? He's just a friend (a good one). You have absolutely nothing to worry about, you know how much I love you and wish you were here. He is funny though, you'd like him. He's kind of like The Beastmaster but a lot funnier. Honestly I have never known anyone put it about so much, he's disgusting. He's been through about fifty odd holiday makers already and I don't think he'll be happy until he reaches triple figures. Let's hope he's using condoms eh?

Hope you are having fun and not missing me too much. I've got about a grand saved now, how much have you managed to save?

Well see you for now, can't wait till we have our own little place. Miss you loads and can't wait to see you.

All my love,
Rachael xxx

Like The Beastmaster, but funnier! Was that supposed to make me feel better? Why not tell me he was like George Clooney, but better looking? Jesus the woman was sharing an apartment with Don fucking Juan. Fifty odd women! I didn't like this, I didn't like this one bit.

Chapter 13

As I anticipated, Sweeney was forgotten about within a week. Life went on, The Beastmaster shagged everyone that got in his way, Scary carried on his award winning impression of The Cowardly Lion and I continued to pillage Bogart's and Tipi's.

Richard proved to be more of a pain in the arse than I anticipated, but the good news was that any future discrepancies in the stocktake would be a shared responsibility. They couldn't just blame me, even if they suspected me. The re-audit was a rather damning indictment of my solo attempt at running the show, but at least it was the last audit before the end of the season, nothing to worry about for the next three months.

My own brush with anxiety attacks never really went any further, and I put the terrifying experience down to the magic mushrooms and the fear of being caught fiddling. I resolved to steer away from acid in future; the panic attacks had at least saved me from one brain-frying narcotic, so it had been a positive thing in one way.

What was more worrying recently was the itching. For the last few days I had been experiencing a constant need to scratch my arms, legs, arse cheeks and back, pretty much everywhere actually. I had checked myself for crabs, which having had them previously I was quite the expert at doing, but there were none. I did however find a strange rash covering most of my body and the gaps between my fingers. At first I attempted to ignore it, hoping it might go away by itself, but eventually I was forced into submission. The memory of the impetigo I had contracted a couple of years ago, the creeping flesh, forced me to visit the camp's medical centre post haste.

My medical card made depressing reading. Well to me anyway. I had been here for just under three years and was in my early twenties, apparently the prime of my life. Yet my medical history made Christopher Reeves look like the very model of vitality. In chronological order it listed, impetigo, gingivitis, pubic lice, non-specific urinary infection, ear and throat infections (two of) and a twisted testicle. This did not even include the two teeth that had simply crumbled on me, they were part of my dental history.

I sat mulling over the medical card; the surgery was unusually empty, just me and Barely Breathing Brian.

'Alright Brian,' I greeted him.

'Alright.'

'Don't tell me you've got a dose, you dirty old buggar.'

'No,' he replied. 'I've come to get some tablets for my depression.'

Jesus, I was sorry I asked. The last thing I needed was to hear this silly old fucker bleating on about how depressed he was. What the fuck was he still doing here anyway? This was no place for someone in their sixties or however old he was. He was staring at me, waiting for me to say something.

'Depression eh? How'd you catch that?'

I watched his mouth move, but didn't hear the words. C'mon doc, where the fuck are you? What's taking so fucking long?

...

'Mr Hisky?'

'That's me,' I said, jumping from my chair.

'Come inside, I'll just have a quick read from your record.'

I said goodbye to Brian and went into the office. The morose looking doctor regarded my medical history. There was no specific camp G.P. The medical centre was staffed by local doctors who rotated the duty. This meant that you rarely got the same guy twice, which saved on embarrassment when you had a card like mine. This one was well into his sixties, with ghostly grey hair and a handlebar moustache, like a brigadier from the Crimean war. Every now and then he would grunt as his tired eyes scanned the white card.

'Well, what seems to be the problem today?' he asked, evidently expecting me to describe symptoms associated with an STD.

'I can't stop itching,' I said.

'Hmmm, whereabouts,' he nodded sagely, no doubt expecting it to be the crabs re-colonizing my pubes.

'Everywhere, my legs, my arms and especially my buttocks.'

'Show me your hands,' he ordered.

I held them out dutifully.

'Well, it looks to me as though you have scabies Mr Hisky.'

'What?'

'Scabies. They are basically parasites that burrow under your skin and lay eggs there, causing an intense itching, like you are experiencing now.'

'So how do I get rid of them?'

'I'll prescribe some cream that you can apply to your whole body. You will have to wash all your clothing and bedding on a high temperature and I will inform your manager that you will have to be medically terminated from today.'

'Medically terminated! Can't I just take a couple of days sick?'

'I am afraid not Mr Hisky. Scabies are highly contagious, we need to avoid a repeat of the outbreaks we have had in the past. You will also need to inform your roommates and they will have to come to see me to make sure that they are not infected. If they are not they will need to change chalets while yours is fumigated. Here is a note for your manager. Good day.'

Fuck me. Fumigated. I had seen these things happening before. Like a scene from The X files or Close Encounters, the men in white suits went in, bringing shame onto the occupants of the chalet that had been diagnosed as harbouring the lurgy. Unclean! Unclean! I felt like crying out. I lit a Mayfair and began wondering bewilderedly towards the management office.

I felt as though the papers I held were for my execution, they may as well have been. Life off camp was no life at all, not as far as I was concerned. Maybe I shouldn't tell anyone. Yes, I could just apply the cream, wash my stuff at the launderette and ask for a chalet transfer. Tell them that The Beastmaster and I had fallen out. Then again, when the spacesuits went in I wanted to be as far away as possible. Plus The Beastmaster would have to move sheds too, otherwise he might think they'd found fucking ET hidden under my bed. Shit, The Beastmaster. That was going to be really hard, letting him know that he too may have the pox. Maybe I would just leave a note.

I entered the management office and prayed it would not be Lorraine. It was.

'Hi Lorraine, I've been sent here by the doctor.'

'I know, he's just phoned me.'

That bastard, he hadn't trusted me. Good job I came clean. Came clean about being unclean.

'So, what do I do now?' I asked.

'I'll give you your termination papers,' she replied. 'Because you are being medically terminated you will receive one extra week's pay as severance.'

'Oh, well that's a relief.' It was. My train fare would be half my week's wage and because the week's severance pay did not have accommodation and food deducted, it was over one hundred and fifty pounds. Maybe this wouldn't be so bad after all. Maybe, I could just spend a week at home, regaining some lost weight, then come back again, once I was fully cured.

'What are the chances of me returning, once I'm cured?' I asked.

'Well, we have already got Richard in Bogart's now and what with the season winding down, I'm not sure we really need two supervisors in one venue.' The fat bitch was scarcely containing her delight.

'I thought you said that Bogart's was too big for one section leader.'

'Yes well, Richard is very experienced, and as I've already said, the season *is* winding down.'

'Aren't there any other section leader positions that need filling?'

'Paul, you know how quickly we fill those positions. You yourself were promoted within a day of Nigel Woodrup being sacked.'

She was right. They didn't hang around when it came to 'making people up', as they called it. I would have been replaced that day, were it not for the fact that they did already have an extra supervisor in the venue.

'What about cook's positions?'

'Paul, why don't you give us a call when you are ready to come back and we'll tell you what's available.'

'Fair enough, thanks,' I conceded. I knew that chubby witch would give me the shittest of jobs if I came back. I'd probably be glass collecting or cleaning bogs. I decided then and there I would try to make it in the real world.

Chapter 14

I lasted three weeks. Three weeks before I realised that I wasn't ready for the real world, or it ready for me. Things had gone fine for the first week or so. I'd got my two week's pay, was signing on sick and eating like a Rwandan lottery winner. After two years without seeing her once even my mother was happy to see me. My clothes no longer stank of sweat and lynx, I washed my hair with shampoo, instead of nineteen pence a bottle washing up liquid and the bathwater actually came above my genitals.

Heaven.

Even the itching seemed to subside, the minute I left camp. This cream was powerful stuff. Wash and go.

The first real snag, was when I went to sign on. I was informed that they had found a job that was ideal for me. A cook, in an American bar and restaurant and in order to receive job seeker's allowance I had to attend any interview that the job centre sent me to.

I dressed down for the occasion, wearing a shirt (but no tie), trousers and black trainers. I arrived about five minutes late, which I reasoned would make a bad impression, without looking intentional.

I hadn't bargained on the manager not even expecting me. He was a tremendously fat man, bald head and sweat stained armpits.

'Sorry, I wasn't made aware by the general manager that anyone was in for an interview today.'

'No problem, would you like me to come back another time?'

'No, no it's fine. Have a seat will you. Would you like a drink?'

'I don't have any money.'

'Nonsense, soft drinks are free to staff here.'

I didn't like the way he said 'to staff'. Christ, this bloke had me on board already, and I hadn't even shown him my (handwritten) CV yet. Slow down tubby, slow down!

'So do you have any experience of working in a busy kitchen?'

'Well...'

...

The job was mine. Tubby (whose real name was Chris) was only too eager to set me on. Even the crossings out on the handwritten CV didn't bother this guy. I had the feeling that he needed bodies, and any old bodies would do. There was no second interview here, he simply handed me a starter pack and told me to fill in the forms while he had some business to attend to in the kitchen. Going to stuff his face no doubt. I was to call on him if I needed any help with the pack.

The starter pack was easy enough to fill out. What sort of muppets did they employ here, if some of them needed help with the form? Still there was one part that I couldn't fill in. The bank details part. I had been under the misguided impression that, like Butlins, all jobs paid in cash. Sure not all on a Monday, like Butlins, but I distinctly remember my dad getting a brown envelope filled with cash every week when I was a kid. Everywhere worked like that, surely.

Apparently not.

The problem I had here was, that in a typically half-witted lack of foresight, especially in view of my numerous County Court Judgments (for bad debts), I had closed down my bank account over two years ago. The reason I perpetrated this act of lunacy was so that I might get at the three pounds forty-five pence that lay within it. In hindsight I should have withdrawn three pounds forty-four pence, leaving a penny behind to keep the account open.

'Er, could you get Chris for me?' I asked the lovely looking blonde waitress as she went past.

'Sure,' she said smiling a perfect set of white teeth that immediately made me self-conscious of my own dental deficiency.

'What's the problem?' Chris asked, dabbing sauce from his mouth as he returned.

'Well, there's a small problem. I don't have any bank details. Is there anyway I could be paid in cash?'

'Oh no. We can't do that. All wages are paid into your bank, by head office. If you need time to set up an account, I can arrange for your first week's pay to be paid by cheque.'

'Ok, that's great. In the meantime I'll try to open up an account. The rest of the forms are filled in.'

'Great, welcome aboard. See you at five o' clock tomorrow evening. Try to get here about ten minutes early so we can arrange your uniform.'

'OK, see you tomorrow.'

I tried every major bank in Leeds. None of them were willing to take me on. I explained that I only wanted a bank account that I could pay money into, no overdraft, no cheque book etc. No joy. I was untouchable. Even the scabies wouldn't be as distasteful to these fucks as my financial past. The one bank that would be willing to touch me, would only offer a savings account, no card, bankbook only, and I had to put in five hundred quid, in order to open it. In the end I returned to the job centre and informed them of the fact that I could not open a bank account, and would not therefore, be able to take the job.

'If you refuse to accept a job, we are not obliged to pay you job seeker allowance.' I was informed by the ferret-faced woman behind the counter.

'So what do you suggest I do?'

'You have family?'

'Yes, my mother, but she can't afford to lend me five hundred pounds.'

'No. You get your wages paid into her account.'

'That seems a little inconvenient.'

'It's either that, or no money at all.'

'Yeah, thanks for all your help,' I said, adding in a lower voice 'ferret face.'

'What was that?'

'I said, thanks for all your help.'

'You're welcome,' she said, coughing into her hand, 'needle dick.'

Chapter 15

The job was shit. No wonder these bastards didn't require a second interview. I was required to work what they called a broiler, which turned out to be a huge barbeque grill. The temperature on that thing had me sweating like Gary Glitter on the internet. On top of the heat everything had to be cooked to order, which required feats of short-term memory far beyond my alcohol ravaged capabilities. Some bloke called Moussa, a Tunisian who bore a remarkable similarity to Colonel Gaddaffi, shouted out the orders as they came in. What an easy job. Just shouting out orders. Why did they give that shit to the Tunisian and the fucking barbeque to me?

I fucked up orders and I fucked up often. Moussa would get real mad, shouting at me and throwing tickets at me when he realised that I was dragging orders from half an hour back.

'Pick up the pace, pick up the pace!' he would shout. 'I need a Chicken Fajita *on the fly!*'

After a couple of weeks of tolerating his tantrums I got sick of the twat and told him to fuck himself, *and* the chicken fajita I was dragging. He gave me a crazy look, picked up a knife and ordered me to step outside. The manager, Chris got wind of the disruption in the kitchen and came to investigate. I could tell just by looking at Chris, that I had fucked with the wrong guy. He didn't want to go anywhere near Moussa while he was waving that big old knife around. As I stood there, trying my best to look undaunted, with Moussa's words echoing around the kitchen: 'I kill before, I kill again!!' or some shit like that.

I thought, na man I'm not ready for the outside world. I took off my apron and walked towards Moussa, trying to look as crazy as possible. He just smiled, as I got closer, licking his lips in anticipation. If I got into a fight with this guy he would no doubt gut me, and show me my insides while I lay there screaming.

'I'll fight you Moussa,' I said, 'just let me go get my fucking knife from the changing rooms.'

'Get knife pig, I fucking kill,' he spat back at me.

'Won't be a moment, I'm gonna fucking enjoy this,' I taunted.

I walked coolly into the changing rooms. People were looking at me in the same way they had looked at Moussa now. Chris, the manager looked as though he was about to keel over. Two psychos were about to have a knife fight on the back dock and every member of staff had abandoned their stations to watch it.

In the changing rooms I pulled off my work boots, put my trainers on and picked up my bag. I walked out, rummaging around the rucksack as though looking for my knife.

'Right then you fucker, outside!' I barked.

Moussa didn't need asking twice he went out onto the back dock and other members of staff started filing out after him, anxious to get a ringside seat. I walked behind them and when everyone was outside, except Chris who just stood there with his head in his hands, I closed the door behind them and bolted it shut, locking all of them out.

'I quit,' I said to Chris, and made a beeline, *on the fly*, for the front exit.

I could hear Moussa's apoplectic cries as he hammered on the locked door, 'I kill, I kill' or some shit like that and I picked up the pace and didn't stop sprinting until I got to the train station.

...

Five days later I called Lorraine.

'Hi Lorraine, It's Whisky.'

'Hello Whisky, what can I do for you?'

'Well, I was wondering if I might be able to return to my old job.'

'I'm afraid we don't really need another section leader at present Whisky. In fact there are no supervisory positions at all at the moment, what with the season winding down.'

'Are there any other positions?' I asked, thinking maybe cook, or bartender.

'Well not really, except for one position in your old venue, Bogart's, but I'm sure that you wouldn't be interested.'

'Well I might be, what's the position?'

'The hot dog cart.'

'...'

'Whisky? Hello.'

'Er, yeah, I can hear you.'

'I didn't think you would be interested. A proud man like you.'

That fucking lard mountain was enjoying this, and I was fairly sure I could hear Julie laughing in the background.

'And you were absolutely right,' I answered. 'If that's all that's available I'm not interested, not interested at all.

Chapter 16

Hiya Whisk,

I can't believe you got medically terminated for having a throat infection. That ice queen, Lorraine, must be getting colder in her old age, the bitch. What's the plan now? Have you had any interviews yet? It's probably for the best really, and I'm actually quite glad you don't intend to go back. I'm sure you'll make a lot more money off camp than you will on and you won't have to put up with people like Knuckles anymore (yes I do remember him. I can't believe he accused you of attacking him, what a prick). I can't believe Sweeney got the chop too, thank god you didn't get implicated. Still his sacking is just one more reason I'm glad you are no longer at that horrible place.

Do me a favour, try not to blow too much of your savings while you are out of work. Just try to think about how nice it will be in our own little place when I get back. God I can't wait to see you, only a few months now before I ravish you.

Things are a bit crap here at moment, have had a falling out with Taylor. The silly sod is selling drugs on the side to supplement his income. Can you believe that? I've told him I don't want him keeping anything in our apartment. Just imagine what would happen if the Spanish police raided the place and found his stash. Cos it doesn't bear thinking about. I'm really upset, as you can imagine.

Anyway, I better get off now. It's really late and I'm on a dolphin spotting tour first thing tomorrow morning.

Can't wait to see you in November,

Miss you loads,

Rachael xxx

I'd had to tell her that I'd been terminated with a throat infection. Scabies wasn't an option, it sounded too much like an STD. I liked the part in her letter about her falling out with Taylor, which was certainly a piece of good news. I didn't need someone like The Beastmaster (but funnier) sniffing round my missus.

My reply was upbeat, probably due to Taylor's fall from grace. I avoided the questions about my savings (there were none) and got down to the nitty gritty, telling her about my brief spell at the American bar and restaurant, and how I would be starting a brand new job in a couple of days.

Chapter 17

The hot dog cart wasn't as bad as it sounded. Demeaning, yes, but there was a great deal of capital to be made pedalling wieners. That twat Richard thought he had his bases covered by counting the sausages before sending me out on my rounds. Each hot dog was supposed to be sold for a pound and he would count out twenty of them and a ten-pound float. I would then be expected to come back with thirty pounds, if I had only twenty-five pounds he would make sure that I also returned with five hot dogs.

What Dickie failed to account for, however, was the awesome inventiveness of the thirsty Butlins' employee. Where there was a will, there was a scam.

'Morning Dale,' I hailed my partner in crime.

'Morning Mr Whisky.'

'Hava you broughta di merchandise?' I asked, affecting a Sicilian accent.

'Si baroni,' I hava di merchandise. Do you hava di, how you say, caaash.'

'Si, si,' I handed him a twenty, while he passed me another opened tin of *No Frills* hot dogs, the third tin he had brought me that day.

'Perfecto, what time is it?'

'Four o' clock.'

'Better make that the last tin then, besides I'm running out of buns here.'

'What time are you going out tonight?' he asked.

'Seven.'

'Do you wanna give me a knock when you finish work or shall I give you the money later?'

'I'll give you a knock,' I said rather hurriedly, knowing that if I left it with him too long it would be drunk or gambled away.

It was a strange feeling, having Dale collect my misappropriated funds, rather than the other way round. He had trusted me to only take a quarter of his takings yet I could not muster up the same faith in him. Perhaps it was the fact that he was infinitely more brutal than I was. I would have liked to keep Dale out of the equation entirely were it not for the possibility of me being searched by Richard on my return to Bogart's.

While I was out and about I was careful to keep the profits from my sideline separate from the official takings. I also took the precaution of selling five or six legit wieners first, so that if any spot checks were made on me I would have some takings and look less suspicious.

All in all I made a tidy return, at fifty-nine pence for a tin of eight *No Frills* dogs my profit margins were excellent. Even allowing for Dale's twenty-five percent I was topping up my beer tokens to the tune of twenty-five quid a day. The best part was that, cock face Richard was so stupid he never even thought to count the bread buns, thereby allowing me to maximise my earning potential.

Chapter 18

Exactly one week after my inglorious return, The
Beastmaster, Scary and I met for a night out. It was the first
time we had been out since I had got back on camp. The
Beastmaster had somehow escaped being infected with the
scabies and had moved in with Scary while the shed was
fumigated. When I returned he moved back into our old shed
with me, leaving Scary with his place to himself again.

It was strictly a beer night, no smoking or acid. Scary had a
habit of doing a Lord Lucan and disappearing when he was
on acid.

We took the bus, which made me strangely nostalgic for
Sweeney. My recent experience of the outside world made
me empathise more with his loss, the poor fucker. I had tried
to phone him while I was at home but his mother informed
me that he was in the clinic. He was no doubt trying to build
up another wad of cash.

Monday nights were always rammed in Skegness for two
reasons; it was payday for Butlins' staff and Fat Louis was a
pound a drink. The only place that you could actually move
in Fat Louis was up by the pool tables, so we took a trip up
there and put a fifty pence piece on the table to book the
next game. There was a shaven headed bloke playing his
girlfriend at the table, barking at her that she was holding
her cue wrong as she attempted to knock in each ball. We
watched them finish the game and then made our way to
rack up the balls.

'Winner stays on mate,' said the shaven headed bloke as I
went to grab his cue.

'Oh, I thought you were finished.'

'Yeah, but it's still winner stays on.'

'Fair enough, you play him if you want Scary.'

'Nah, Whisk, it's all right. You go first.'

'We can play doubles if you want?' the skinhead suggested. 'Fiver a man.'

'I'm not playing for money,' I replied.

'No come on Whisk,' The Beastmaster whispered to me. 'I'll stump up the money and play with you. Did you see how shit she was, it's an easy fiver each. That's five pints tonight mate.'

'OK, we'll play doubles. A fiver a man,' I conceded.

'Let me just get my partner,' he replied, walking straight past his girlfriend towards the bar.

Fuck me, I thought, we're being hustled here. This bloke's probably got Paul Newman for a partner. My mouth dropped as he returned with my old friend Knuckles in tow.

'Well, well,' an extremely pissed looking Knuckles laughed, as he swaggered up to the table. 'Look who it is.'

'Matt,' I greeted him, thankful that there were three of us and only two of them.

'What we playing for?' he slurred. 'Tenner a man?'

'No, a fiver,' I replied.

'A fiver? I'm not playing for a poxy fiver. Tenner a man, come on.'

'We're playing for a fiver,' I repeated.

'Fucking poofs,' came his reply.

'OK mate,' The Beastmaster jumped in. 'We'll take your money from you.'

I stared at him, questioningly, but he simply winked as if to say it was easy money. The Beastmaster was pretty good at pool, but I wasn't, plus we had no idea what these two played like.

I didn't like it.

We flipped for the break, which they won. The skinhead broke the balls and potted two stripes in doing so. Great start. He then sank another three stripes in a row, before missing the next. The Beastmaster stepped up ahead of me and quickly sank four spots, before accidentally potting the white.

Knuckles took the table, staggering around drunkenly as he did so and wasting his two shots. Unbelievably I then sank three of our balls, setting myself up for the black. The Beastmaster *was* right to take the bet. I was going to get one up on Knuckles. I hammered the black into the back pocket, then watched in horror, as the white went into the middle one.

'YEEESSSS!' shouted Knuckles. 'Get off my fucking table man!'

'Unlucky mate,' Scary said, patting my back as he did so.

'Double or quits,' The Beastmaster demanded.

'I'm not playing double or quits,' I told him.

'Come on mate. We can easily beat them,' he whispered. 'Have you seen how pissed Knuckles is? They got lucky.'

'I don't care. I'm not playing for another tenner and neither should you.'

'Carey, will you play?'

'No. Sorry mate, but I always fuck up when I play for money.'

'I thought I told you losers. Get off my fucking table!' Knuckles taunted again.

The Beastmaster didn't look happy at all. He glared at Knuckles, who simply waved the tenner he had just won in front of The Beastmaster's face.

'I'll tell you what,' The Beastmaster declared. 'Double or quits, that my dick can reach the bottom of this beer glass on the slack.'

'What?' Knuckles asked incredulously.

'I said, double or quits that my fucking knob can reach the bottom of this beer glass, on the slack.'

'Yeah, keep dreaming gay lord. You just want some excuse to get your dick out in front of a bunch of blokes.'

'If I did fancy blokes I would fancy real ones, not a cock-less twat like you.'

'You'll be fucking cock-less soon, you cunt, I'll fucking rip yours off if you're not careful.'

'OK then, if I reach the bottom of the glass we're all square. If however I can't, you can give me a kick in the bollocks.'

'You're fucking on,' yelled Knuckles. 'If you don't reach the bottom you get a kick in the bollocks and your mate owes mine twenty quid, instead of ten.'

'Fuck me mate, do you know what you're doing?' I asked. 'That pint glass is about eight inches deep, you can't reach that on the slack.'

'Watch me.'

The Beastmaster seemed confident enough. The twisted fucker must have practised this in his room, I thought. A small crowd gathered round, mainly girls, as he began to unbutton his jeans.

'Fucking hell mate you don't have to do a striptease you know,' Knuckles scoffed.

'Well I'm not gonna do it through my fly am I? I'll loose a couple of centimetres that way,' he replied.

There were gasps and giggles from the girls as he pulled his boxers down to reveal his colossal cock. The Beastmaster smiled and winked in the direction of the ladies, before massaging it in order to stretch it to its optimum length.

'Hey no wanking. You said on the slack,' shouted Knuckles, evidently a little flustered now that he had witnessed the majesty of The Beastmaster's appendage.

'I'm not wanking knob head. If that's how you wank I'd hate to see how you fuck,'

The Beastmaster took the Guinness glass and began to lower his cock and bollocks into it. I was sure he would reach the bottom and he looked fairly confident himself. He must have tried it before, he must have. Then again, maybe not. He was a good centimetre short. Fuck.

'Whehey, pay up you fucking loser,' Knuckles taunted, as I handed his mate another tenner. 'And you, I hope you know a good doctor, cause I used to be a goalkeeper and I could kick the ball all the way to the opposite six yard box.'

The Beastmaster had turned a funny colour and appeared oblivious to the commotion around him.

'Right, outside cunt!' Knuckles shouted, heading towards the exit.

'Yeah, yeah, just let me go for a piss first. I might be too sore after you kick me in the fucking bollocks mind.'

'Go on then you cunt, but if you're not back in five minutes I'll take it out on your mate here.'

'Don't worry, I'll be back,' he said heading for the toilets.

...

When he failed to reappear ten minutes later, Knuckles and I realised that The Beastmaster had given us the slip. Ordinarily this would have been an excellent turn of events. However, with Knuckles' words still fresh in my mind, I knew that The Beastmaster's no-show would mean a serious amount of pain, boarding an express shuttle bound for my gonads. Next stop unoch city. All aboard!

Knuckles was becoming increasingly agitated as the minutes went by, constantly reminding us all what he was going to do if The Beastmaster didn't show.

'I'm gonna take it out on him. I am, I'm gonna take it out on him,' he kept repeating while pointing at me. By now Knuckles and the skinhead had been joined by another two of their Skegness mates, who held Scary and I back to prevent us from escaping.

'Look Matt, he's paid you his twenty quid. You got your money, why don't we just leave it there,' suggested Scary,

who until now had been a silent spectator in the whole
episode.

'Yeah well, you should have said that to your mate when
he started to shoot his fucking mouth off shouldn't you?'

'Like you said, it was The Beastmaster that was shooting
his mouth off, why don't you take it up with him next time
you see him? Whisky's paid his twenty quid, he doesn't owe
you anything.'

'Oh, I'll take it up with him next time I see him, and I'm
sure your girlfriend Whisky will after I've kicked his
bollocks into his stomach.'

'You're not touching his bollocks. That was The
Beastmaster's bet.'

'Look, if you're not careful I'll do the fucking same to you,
you big fucking ape. Stay out of this or you'll end up
li...UGGGHH!!'

The blow knocked Knuckles straight to the ground, his
head hit the kerb and his backward momentum flung his legs
into the air as he sat on his back. The punch was awesome,
like a boxer on angledust. Goodnight Knuckles, we wouldn't
be hearing from him again, but in an instant the other three
were on us. I went down onto my back after a few punches
from one of the Skeg lads, who then began putting the boot
in. As he did so I spun around on the floor with my legs
flailing in the air, like a breakdancer with a bad back, trying
to keep him away from me. Scary had smacked another of
the lads and was currently grappling with the skinhead when
I looked across.

When he got the better of him he got up and shouted to my
assailant: 'Come on then you fucking cunt!'

Jesus, he was like a madman. I had forgotten what an
awesome antagonist Scary could make, while on beer. I was
so used to him jumping at his own shadow while on drugs.
My attacker was backing off now, eyeing his three mates on
the floor. It looked like a scene from the chronicles of Des

Bailey. The quarry had turned on the predators and they were fucked.

'Come on mate let's go,' said Scary, keeping his eye on the remaining Skeg lad.

'I'm coming, don't worry,' I said, and as he helped me up. We turned and began to run in the direction of camp.

We had gotten about a couple of hundred meters down the road when we heard the sound of police sirens heading in the direction of Fat Louis.

'Shit,' said Scary. 'We better split up. I'm gonna follow the beach down, you get a taxi and I'll see you back at camp.'

'OK mate, see you later. Oh and Scary, thanks. Thanks a lot mate.'

'No bother, you'd do the same for me.'

'Well I'm not so sure about that,' I said.

'Yeah, you would,' he nodded, and turned to run for the beach.

Chapter 19

As I watched Scary jog into the distance, I realised that
after losing all my cash to Knuckles, I might not have
enough left to pay for the three-mile taxi journey home. I
dug into my pockets and counted the collection of silver and
copper coins that lay within, two pounds twelve pence.
Fuck.

The fare was usually around four quid, which meant I
could either walk the first leg of the journey and flag down a
cab, or walk the last leg. I reasoned that by walking the first
leg I was less likely to come across Knuckles and his cronies
back in town on my way to the taxi rank. Secondly if I
walked the first leg, someone that knew me may well spot
me and get their taxi to pull over -thus saving my money for
a pint at last orders in the staff club.

Logic won the day and I began the first leg of my journey
on foot, sticking close to the road so that any passing
associates might see me. I reasoned that Knuckles and his
pals were more likely to be in an ambulance to the hospital
than a taxi heading for camp. Therefore I was unlikely to be
jumped by them this evening.

About a mile down the road I realised that what had started
out as a mild urge to empty my bowels had now, either due
the Newcastle Brown or the fear from my scrape with
Knuckles, become an urgent, cloth browning, need to take a
dump.

Looking around I spotted a wall that looked low enough to
jump over yet high enough to take a shit behind. I hurdled
the wall and quickly pulled down my trousers and pants.
Strange noises emanated from my arse and a gush of liquid
brown adrenaline shot out, burning my sphincter as it
covered a large area of grass around me. I had forgotten how
pissed I actually was and now that the sobering adrenaline
was gushing from my arse I began to stagger around, falling

over as my pants restricted my ankles. I picked myself up,
grabbed a handful of grass and made a cursory wipe around
my arsehole. I then, rather clumsily, fell over again, before
scrambling over the wall onto the main road.

Another mile down the road I thought I might be close
enough to camp for a couple of quid to get me home and
began attempting to flag down a taxi. Eventually one
stopped about twenty meters in front of me. I jogged up to
the front door and opened it.

'Evening mate,' I said as I turned to lower myself onto the
front seat.

While I was lowering myself in, the taxi driver screeched
off, almost throwing me back onto the kerb.

'Hey watch out you mad bastard, stop taking the piss?' I
yelled.

The driver didn't answer; he pulled over again about ten
meters away and leaned over to close his door properly.

'FUCKING DICKHEAD!' I screamed, before trudging off
again, holding out my thumb for any other cabs that went
by.

None stopped and I cursed my luck as I got closer and
closer to camp. By the time I reached the security gates I
knew I had missed last orders at the staff bar and that I
might as well head straight back to my chalet. I showed my
card to the security guard at the gate and headed home. I was
vaguely aware of the old bastard chuckling as I staggered
away, but put that down to my erratic sideward movements
as I wobbled towards my shed.

When I finally reached the sanctuary of the chalet, I went
straight to my room and fell over a couple more times as I
struggled to remove my clothing. It was at this point that I
began to notice a rank stench that felt thick enough to chew
on. Jesus, what was this on my jeans? They were covered. It
looked like...yes it was...well at least it smelled like...shit!
No wonder that fucking taxi driver had shot off. That's why

the security bloke was laughing. I had fallen over into my own shit, while I was spraying it onto the grass. Jesus that smelled bad. I had to get rid of these fucking Levi's and I had to do it tonight.

Chapter 20

It was a rude awakening to say the least. I was used to the sound of girls' screaming coming from The Beastmaster's room, but not from the toilet.

'AGGGHHHRR!!!' it went, waking me suddenly from my catatonic condition. My first thoughts were that he was raping someone, until I heard her shout him for help, 'CRAIG! CRAIG HELP! COME QUICK!'

I heard his door open and I heard him cursing, 'Jesus..Oh God...What the fuck...Come on let's get out of here.'

'Hey! Keep it down out there! I'm trying to fucking sleep here,' I shouted. I was in no mood to be woken by that treacherous twat, after he had very nearly cost me a kicking.

'Whisky, I'm serious man. We need to get out of this fucking chalet.'

'Why? What is it? A fire?'

'No man.'

'Then shut the fuck up.'

'Listen mate, this is just as serious as fire.'

'What the hell could be as serious as a fire?'

'Shit!'

'What?' I said, jolting into full consciousness as I remembered the jeans.

'The bog's blocked. It's overflowing. There's turds everywhere. We've got to get out. You'd better put your shoes on before you leave your room.'

I jumped out of bed and hurriedly put on some clothes, and shoes. I opened the door to my room and was met with an apocalyptic sight. The stench hit me first, like a blitzkrieg on my nostrils, then the scene of devastation revealed itself. The whole of the floor was soaked in water, lumps of shit and toilet roll were floating, like foul islands in an offensive ocean of piss and bog water. Oddly, the clumps of bog roll were not just the white stuff that we stole from the various pub toilets on camp but there were pink, blue and yellow pieces too. Other peoples used shit roll!

'Come on Whisky,' shouted The Beastmaster.

'I..I can't.'

'You have to. Come on take my hand,' he shouted, as though he was Sly Stallone in *Cliffhanger*.

'Fuck off, I'll just go out my window.'

'Fair enough,' he conceded, as I climbed out the window. 'I think we'd better get down to the accommodation office.'

…

It wasn't long before we found out. A man in a blue boiler suit, who looked like he had done battle with many a turd in his Butlins career, solved the mystery for us. He looked like the Dirty Harry of the plumbing world, 'I know what you're thinking. Did I find six lumps of shit in the U bend, or only five?' He emerged triumphantly from our chalet holding a number of pieces of what appeared to be stained brown rags.

'Some idiot has cut up a pair of Jeans, Levi's, and flushed them down the bog,' he declared. 'The toilet pipes have then become blocked and anything flushed from the eight surrounding chalets has hit the blockage point and been forced up through the only outlets it could find, namely the cisterns of chalets Y1 and X1.'

X1 was the chalet behind ours, inhabited by two male dancers from The Showboat, one of whom was repeatedly vomiting as the other rubbed his back. The Beastmaster and I were evidently made from sterner stuff than the occupants of this chalet.

'It's OK Sebastian. It's OK.'

'But who would do such a thing?' enquired Sebastian.

'God knows, it could be any one of eight chalets.'

'Oh Timothy please, let's move off camp. We could get a condominium in town...or commute from Lincoln.'

'Sebastian, you know we can't afford that on these wages.'

'But I really don't know how much longer I can stand this place Timothy. Really, I'm an artist. I'm emotionally drained.'

'Come on Sebastian, we'll go into town for a cappuccino. That will make you feel better.'

'Can we at least look at some estate agencies while we are there?'

'Of course we can my love, of course we can.'

We watched them leave arm in arm, The Beastmaster turned to me and shook his head.

'They've got a point though. Who would do such a thing? Do you reckon that Knuckles did it to punish me for running off?'

'He's got other things to worry about believe you me.'

'Like what?'

'Scary knocked him out last night.'

'What?'

'You heard. Scary knocked him out. I wouldn't be surprised if he doesn't get some sort of warning from Des. You know he takes a dim view on his staff fighting around town.'

'Go on Scary. I wish I'd seen that.'

'Yeah, well, you would've seen that if you hadn't gone and left us in the shit.'

'You can hardly blame me; didn't you notice that he was wearing steel toe capped boots?'

'Yep, and he very nearly used them on me thanks to you doing a runner.'

'Nah, you paid up man, he wouldn't have done you. It's me that he's after.'

'Well, he's not the only one who's after you now.'

'What do you mean?'

'Scary. He wasn't too chuffed with you after you abandoned us last night. I'd watch myself if I were you.'

This was bullshit. Scary would never hurt The Beastmaster, but I was enjoying watching him squirm as I told him. He looked warily over his shoulder, as if worried that Scary was behind him.

'What did he say?'

'Just that he'd be seeing you later.'

'Ah, he'll be all-right,' he said, but he didn't look convinced.

Chapter 21

When I arrived at work that afternoon, Dale was working on the counter instead of being over in the ice cream parlour at the pool. He was listening to Richard explain how the till worked in Bogart's and looked thoroughly pissed off. I looked at him quizzically and he shrugged his shoulders in resignation. Richard turned to me with a big smile on his face; I could tell he had some bad news.

'Lorraine would like to see you,' he said.

'When?'

'Now.'

'Any reason?'

'Don't ask me Whisky, just get yourself over to the office and all will be revealed.'

I was in no hurry to get over to the lard mountain's office and took my time, stopping to chain smoke two cigarettes over a game of pinball in the amusements on the way. When I did arrive at the office, I knocked at the door and shifted my weight from heel to heel as I waited for that poisonous bitch to summon me in.

'Enter,' she called.

'Hi Lorraine. Richard said you wanted to see me.'

'Yes, congratulations Whisky, you're being promoted.'

'Promoted? I thought we had enough section leaders.'

'We do. You are being promoted to chef, in Bogart's.'

'Chef? They already have a chef.'

'Not anymore. Andy is being moved over to The Showboat, as that's where most of the business will take place in the forthcoming weekend breaks. Tipi's and the hot dog bike are being closed down and so we will be moving Dale into Bogart's to take over from Stacey on the counter, while you will be the new chef.'

'Do I have any choice?'

'Well you could resign, but other than that...no.'

'When does this take effect?'

'Now. You know Bogart's as well as anybody. Andy won't even have to train you up. You are the ideal candidate. Besides, I thought you would be happy, it's an extra ten pounds per week.'

Ten pounds a week my bollocks, I would be losing about twenty five quid a day if I lost the hot dog cart, not to mention the loss of revenue that Dale's transfer would incur. Shit. Fuck. I had no choice, it was chef or nothing, the bike was going to be closed down anyway. I'd just have to think of a new way to bring the coin in.

'Oh, by the way,' the bitch added as I made to leave. 'There's a letter for you in Bogart's' pigeon hole.'

'Cheers.'

Chapter 22

Whisky,

My god, I can't believe you went back there! Are you mad? Jesus Whisky, you need to tear yourself away from that shit hole. Think about it, you would have probably had a steady job by the time I got back. That way we wouldn't have to worry about us both being out of work and looking for jobs at the same time.

Still, if that's what you want to do with your life, then fair enough. Don't let me stop you. I just hope you don't intend to spend another winter there, because I personally never want to see Butlins again after the 18-30's reunion. Seriously Whisky, you have got a degree and you're working on a hot dog bike, I'm starting to wonder if you have any ambition at all.

Take care,

Rachael.

  No kisses on this letter eh? No missing you either, well fuck her.
  My reply was blunt. No ambition? I was a cook now, not a bloody hot dog salesman. And who was she to talk anyway? As if getting pissed for a living and producing rude versions of *Jack and the Beanstalk* represented ambition. If she wanted someone with *those* type of aspirations maybe she should be trying to patch things up with her precious Taylor. She might even get her drugs free from him too.

Chapter 23

With Richard breathing down our necks it was hard to think up any elaborate, money-making scams that did not involve a high risk of being caught. I had three years invested in this place and had recently had a taste of how overrated life was on the outside of camp. I wasn't willing to take any great risks. I'd minesweep my booze if I had to, it was good enough for my predecessor and it would be good enough for me. Dale on the other hand, didn't care about being sacked, he just wanted money and he wanted it now.

Within a few hours, while Richard was attending to his paperwork in the office, we had worked out our first scam. It couldn't involve leaving extra money in the till, or taking the money and building it back up. The money had to go straight from the customer to our pockets, bypassing the till altogether on the way. I was a chef, I didn't work a till and as such I would be less likely to be searched for money by any suspicious security staff or managers. Our scam was simple. We kept a number of one penny pieces at the side of the till. Most items cost one or two pounds and ninety-nine pence. Anyone paying for a one pound ninety-nine burger with two pound coins would, with our scam, be given a penny change from the side of the till. The two quid would then be quickly passed to me.

The problem with the scam was that it relied on the customer paying with almost exact change. It also meant a fifty-fifty cut on takings, which seemed to bother Dale a great deal more than it bothered me. After a week of running the scam we had made about twenty quid each, which was chicken feed compared to our takings beforehand. In addition to this, Richard seemed to have a knack of always being around when the lucrative customers were paying. Why he couldn't just stay in his office drinking or something, like I used to do, was beyond me.

...

Eventually, after a number of barren shifts, an opportunity for Dale to make some real money presented itself. The shop was empty and we were just beginning to unwind from the stress of twenty minutes reasonably hard work, when Dale looked at the counter and spotted something.

'Hey what's that?' he asked. 'It looks like a purse.'

'It is,' I replied, as I took it from the counter and made my way towards the office.

'Where the fuck are you going?'

'To put it in the safe, until the owner comes back.'

'You're fucking not! Pass it here. Don't you even want to know how much is in there?'

'Well not really, I'm sure the owner will be back when she realises it's missing.'

'That could be hours, she might not even remember where she lost it.'

'That's not a risk I want to take.'

'Just pass me the fucking purse,' he said, malevolently.

I held it out and he snatched it from my hand, his eyes glaring at me as he opened it. When he looked down into the purse his eyes lit up as if he'd discovered the crown jewels in there.

'Fucking hell!' he exclaimed. 'There must be about two hundred quid in here...and what's this...huh, it's a winning scratch card...for another fifty quid. You fucking dancer.'

'Dale, she's bound to come back. If she says she left it here and we get searched by security, we're screwed.'

Dale screwed his face up as though the process of thinking actually hurt him. Then he lit up again.

'I've got it,' he hissed. 'We give it twenty minutes, if she hasn't come back, I go on my break and hide the purse. That way, if she does come back later, we won't have the purse on us.'

'If you've been on your break in the meantime, they'll search your chalet.'

'I'll hide it somewhere else.'

'Where?'

'You leave that to me sunshine,' he replied, tapping his nose. 'You leave that to me.'

Twenty minutes passed and no one had come back to the store. I didn't want any part of this, but I knew that Dale would not take no for an answer. I didn't like the thought of stealing a purse and resolved to stay out of it. He could keep the money. I wouldn't grass, that would be suicidal, but I wouldn't take a penny of that money.

Dale went to see Richard in the office to ask if he could take his break, he could. He winked at me as he went out, with a huge grin on his face. I returned a narrow lipped smile and knew, just fucking knew, that there would be trouble ahead

...

There *was* trouble ahead, and when it came in, an hour later, it came in hysterically. She was only around twenty years old, short, blonde and pretty, accompanied by her boyfriend, who appeared to be about the same age. They approached the counter, where I was leaning chatting to Dale, looking extremely concerned.

'Has anyone handed in a purse?' she asked, half crying as she did so.

'NO!' Dale replied quickly, before I could say anything.

'But, I'm sure I left it here. I haven't taken it out of my handbag anywhere else.'

'Sorry love, no-one's handed one in,' Dale reiterated, pretending to look around the counter. 'Maybe it's dropped on the floor somewhere...No, not here, how about that side Whisky?'

'Errr, nothing here, no.'

'But it must be. I'm telling you, this is the only place I've used it. It must be here. Is there a manager around?'

'There's no manager in here,' Dale answered.

'Come on Charlotte, we'll have another look in the chalet,' her boyfriend suggested.

'IT'S NOT THERE!' she cried. 'IT'S HERE. SOMEONE'S TAKEN IT. I LEFT IT IN HERE. I WANT TO SEE A MANAGER!'

'Where can I find a manager?' the boyfriend asked us, while stroking her shoulders to comfort her.

'There is an office over by the bookmakers on the other side of camp. It's the one with the sign saying Food and Beverage Management.'

'And there's no manager here?'

'No, only a supervisor, he's in his office, busy,' Dale informed him.

'Well I'd like to speak to him anyway.'

'Fair enough. I'll just go get him,' Dale replied, coolly, but I could tell he was riled. He glared at me as he went back to the office to get Richard and I followed him back there.

'Not a fucking word,' he whispered, pointing a threatening finger as we made our way through. What he didn't say, but his voice implied was, 'or you're fucking dead.'

By the time Richard came out, the girl was wailing hysterically again and looking at us accusingly, as though we had murdered her child or something. He asked us to go wait in the kitchen as he dealt with the problem. We duly obliged, but stayed within earshot of the counter so that we could hear what was said.

I wished I hadn't, the girl sobbed uncontrollably and pretty much accused the two of us of robbing her purse. I felt a strange sense of injustice that this woman had the audacity to accuse me of something without any proof, but then laughed at the irony of the fact that she was actually quite correct.

Dale was looking very concerned by now. I could tell it wasn't concern about being accused, or even being searched. He was worried that I would break and grass him up. As we strained to hear the conversation he glared at me the whole time. His eyes looked black, full of malevolence, weighing me up.

'What we gonna do?' I whispered, breaking the silence.

'We're not gonna do anything. We just leave it a few days and we share out the money,' he replied, as though we were great train robbers or something. I half expected him to tell me not to go buying anything flash.

'You keep the money,' I told him. 'I don't want any.'

'You're fucking taking it,' came the reply. 'I don't want you getting any funny ideas; you're just as much a part of this as I am.'

There was no arguing. Dale had spoken. I had to take half that cash whether I wanted to or not. I hated the cunt now. I had always been happy to boost my income at the expense of the company. Shit, I felt it was a duty at times; after all they were exploiting us, milking us, feeding us gruel and housing us in asbestos coated cardboard boxes. Providing beds no larger than an ironing board and sheets that were twenty years old. They'd even toyed with the idea of paying us in Butlins vouchers at one point so that all our income had to be re-spent on camp. I had no moral objections to taking from this firm, but stealing that girl's purse, that wasn't me. I wanted no part of that. Maybe I would grass this fucker up. Maybe I'd knock his teeth down his throat, teach him a lesson he'd not soon forget. But maybe I'd just do as I was told.

Chapter 24

I did as I was told. We were searched, of course, by Knuckles and one of his workmates. We feigned indignation. Dale was particularly convincing, even accusing the girl of fraud. 'Have you taken out travel insurance by any chance?' he grilled her. 'I don't want to loose my job so that you can put in a false claim.'

'Shut up!' said Knuckles as he led Dale off into the office to search him.

'I want you to be present at my search,' I said to Richard. 'That security guard has got it in for me. I don't want him planting anything on me.'

'Fair enough,' said Richard. 'I am going to have to report this to the management, regardless of the outcome, you do understand?'

'Yes, of course.'

He wasn't so bad, I thought. Bit of a geek, yes, but he was fair and honest and you couldn't really ask for more in a boss. Maybe if I'd been a bit more like him I might have been in management by now. I had some brains, a degree even, only third class (and without honours) but that could easily have been a 2:1 or 2:2 if I had actually done some revision instead of boozing and playing pool. I felt myself becoming morose, turning to introspection. So promising a young student reduced to riding a hot dog bike or stealing handbags. This wasn't how it was supposed to be. I had once dreamt of becoming a novelist or failing that something exciting, like a fireman. As I stood there waiting to be strip searched by a security guard that hated me, lamenting the way my life had turned out, I realised that this is how those redcoats must feel every day. Some of those guys did have talent. There were some good singers and performers among that crew. Like Sweeney had said, they had probably dreamed of becoming actors or pop stars, nobody dreams of becoming a redcoat. Yet everyday they were forced into the indignity of pulling on that stupid red and white clown's outfit, their hot dog bike, and having to keep a bunch of miserable brats entertained. No wonder this camp was awash with mind-bending drugs. No wonder we all drank like our liver was our worst enemy. The reality was just too hard to bear. That's what this place was. A graveyard. A graveyard of lost hopes.

Chapter 25

The problem with having such a psychotic acquaintance as Dale Fortune is that it's hard to turn them down when they ask for something. So when Dale knocked on my door at eleven in the morning four days later, suggesting a pre-work drinking session, I had a major dilemma. Here was a session that I could do without, but saying no to Dale wasn't an easy proposition.

I dragged myself out of bed and threw on some clothes.

'Are you going to the canteen first?' I asked him.

'Fuck that,' he replied.

I wasn't about to argue.

Dale had chosen The Swinging Shilleleigh, Butlins', Irish theme pub. It is important to record here that the extent of this pub's Irishness was something akin to that of spaghetti, that is to say there was nothing Irish about it whatsoever. They didn't even sell Guinness for pity's sake. Can you imagine an Irish theme pub without Guinness?

What they did sell however, like every other bar on Butlins, regardless of theme, was Beamish.

'Let's have a drop of the black stuff,' Dale suggested as we entered the pub. He then shouted to the barmaid, 'Play *Wild Rover* will you Leanne?'

Leanne obliged by pouring two pints of Beamish and putting a CD named *Twenty Classic Irish Folk Songs* into the sound system, and skipping to track nine.

The sound system struggled to compete in volume with the over zealous crooning of that most patriotic of Irishmen, Dale Fortune.

'I SPENT ALL ME MONEY ON WHISKEY AND BEER!!' he sang.

Behind us I was vaguely aware of two new punters entering the bar, and only realised that it was Emma Huntley, the Food and Beverage Executive, and her assistant when they stood beside me and said hello.

'Oh hi Emma, hi Lucy,' I greeted them.

'Hi Paul, day off today?' Emma replied.

I had to lie. With this fuckwit singing away next to me, I couldn't claim I was just having a quiet pint before work. Besides Dale was just in the middle of ordering a couple of Jameson whiskey chasers as I struggled for an answer.

'Yeah, how about you?' I asked.

'Yeah, first day off in two weeks,' Emma replied. 'What you drinking?'

'Beamish.'

'And Irish whiskey,' Dale butted in. 'Leanne another two whiskeys for the lovely ladies please.'

Leanne responded by pouring another two whiskeys out and placing them in front of Emma and Louise. I could tell that she felt awkward. This was probably due to the fact that her boss was drinking at her bar, which meant she would have to make herself look busy. But there was also the fact that until Emma and Lucy had walked in; she would have been providing us with either reduced price or free drinks, as was customary between friends, especially friends working for two quid an hour. With the arrival of Emma and Lucy she would now have to ask for the full retail value.

'Nine pounds sixty for the four Jamesons,' Leanne informed Dale.

'Fuckin' hell, nine sixty!' Dale exclaimed as he dug out a tenner note from his pocket. 'Keep the change love.'

'Thanks,' Leanne replied.

'So, what you planning to do with your rest day?' I asked Emma in an attempt at light conversation.

'Probably just have a few in here and then go into Skegness,' she replied.

'Come on drink up, it's your round next!' Dale shouted, shaking his empty whiskey glass at Emma.

'Er, perhaps we should get off in a minute Dale,' I

suggested.

'Fuck that, it's Emma's round, come on Emma, don't be tight, you must be on about six times my wage.'

'Let's get off mate,' I reiterated, widening my eyes, as if suggesting that getting drunk with the management, shortly before shift, might not be the best idea.

'No, he's right,' Emma interrupted. 'You guys work hard, and for very little money. I'll get them in. Four Jamesons please Leanne, and four pints of Beamish too.'

Oh God, I thought. I knew that this would not end well. The clap of thunder that rumbled outside was an appropriate accompaniment to Emma's random act of kindness. I knew that Lucy was bound to follow her boss' lead and order another round after this one and I knew that by then, Dale would be on a roll and end up completely ratted by the time he started work.

'Christ, it's really coming down out there,' Lucy noted.

Looking out the huge window, past the stencilled lettering on the pane, proclaiming there to be 'good craic' found within, I spied the rain coming down like a Mumbai monsoon. People were darting around, seeking the nearest available shelter.

Fuck me, I thought, I hope this isn't in for the day. We'll never get out of the pub.

...

Two hours later, *Wild Rover* was playing for the dozenth time that day and Dale, Emma and Lucy were all banging their whiskey glasses on the bar in accompaniment. I sat quietly regarding the river of rain that was now collecting under the tunnel leading to the staff quarters, and Bogart's. I knew that the flood was bad in one respect, i.e. I would have to wade through the tunnel in order to get home and to work; yet good in another, there would be little or no chance of any management crossing through the tunnel in its flooded condition. This meant that the only person of any authority that would see our drunken condition at work would be Richard, who was proving to be rather spineless on the disciplinary front.

'I'm off,' I eventually announced. 'You coming Dale?'

'No, I'm gonna stay here for another hour.'

There was no point arguing. Dale sneered in the face of responsibility, especially when half tanked.

'Alright mate, I'll see you later,' I said.

I alighted from my bar stool, left the dry sanctuary of The Swinging Shilleleigh, and headed toward the tidal lagoon that had settled in the underpass. Some bright spark had hit upon the idea of using beer crates, turned upside down, to make a makeshift bridge across the body of water. Unfortunately at its deepest point the crates failed to reach the bottom and consequently were floating rather than standing firm. I discovered this when I jumped onto one and toppled off it, straight into the water.

'Fuck me!' I screamed as the freezing water completely soaked me. A small crowd of holidaymakers burst into hysterical laughter, as I got up and waded the rest of the way to the other side.

'Nobody panic! I'm all right!' I shouted to them in a small attempt at making light of my situation. They all cheered and a couple of the girls among them bit their bottom lips out of embarrassment for me.

Oh well, I thought, at least the plunge sobered me up somewhat, and fortunately there were not *too* many people around to witness my shame. I shook myself off and ran home to get a bath and ready for work.

...

My shift started at five and Dale was due to start at half past, however at quarter to six there was still no sign of him.

'You seen Dale today?' Richard asked.

'Er, I saw him earlier, but not since two o' clock.'

'Ok, I'll get one of the bar staff to go give his chalet a kno…What the fuck?' Richard exclaimed, staring out of the window with his mouth wide open.

I looked out the window towards the flooded tunnel opposite the shop. Over in the tunnel, an extremely pissed looking Dale was ferrying people across the water by means of a piggyback. The eternal entertainer, he then proceeded in an attempt to do the backstroke in the puddle, which was about two feet deep.

'I don't fucking believe it,' said Richard. He actually sounded quite angry, which was unusual for him. 'Is that Dale?'

'Er, I think so,'

'DALE!' Richard shouted, as he made his way outside, 'You're supposed to be at work at half past five.'

Wow, Dickie was actually showing some backbone here, not like him at all. This might mean trouble for Dale. I followed outside to listen in.

'Chill out man!' Dale called back, climbing out of the water and heading towards Richard.

'Don't tell me to chill out, you loser, what the hell do you think you are playing at? Go get a bath and changed for work. And brush your teeth you stink of b..,'

I meant to ask Richard later, whether he was about to say booze, or beer, maybe even Beamish, before he received a mouthful of Dale's fist.

'You're the one whose breath stinks. From all that arse lickin' you slimy fucking poof!' he announced as he stood over Richard.

No answer. Richard wisely adopted to stay quiet, and down, rather than risk a further beating. He waited until Dale retreated off to his chalet before picking himself off the floor and dialling the number for Lorraine's office.

'Yeah, I think you had better come over here,' I heard him say over the phone, 'Yes, it's important.'

I guess Lorraine didn't fancy traversing that bloody puddle.

Chapter 26

Where Dale was dangerous, his replacement was downright disgusting. She was a forty-four year old woman, named Diane. It wasn't just her face that disgusted me, though it had more than a passing resemblance to a ferret licking vinegar from a nettle, but everything about her. The way she waddled when she walked reminded me of a particularly awkward football mascot. If somehow the halitosis that polluted her each and every exhale could have been concentrated and bottled, it would have constituted a major development in biological warfare, a new and terrifying terrorist threat. Miraculously this woman had somehow persuaded three men to marry her. Beastmasters three, a trio of dragon-layers.

'Evening Whisky,' she screeched, as I entered the kitchen.

'Evening Di,' I replied, shuddering as I wondered how her husband, that desperado Jeremy, could possibly bring himself to shag someone as grotesque as her.

'Do you think we'll be busy tonight?' she asked.

Busy trying to avoid any close contact with you, you sickening old hag, I thought.

'Yeah, probably.'

'That's a shame. My bunions are giving me hell.'

Oh dear god, bring Dale back I implore you. I'll do anything; I'll suck your holy dick.

'Right, I'm off into the kitchen. I've got a lot of prepping up to do.'

'Ok see you later love.'

Don't call me love you decrepit bitch, I wanted to scream.

'Yeah see you.'

This was disastrous. Weekend breaks were almost upon us and I was stuck in the arsehole of camp, flipping burgers and frying chicken with lunch lady Doris from *The Simpsons*. I needed to engineer a move to The Showboat. That's where the action was on weekend breaks. That's where all the best DJ's would be playing on the 18-30's reunion. That's where the fanny was at and maybe where Rachael would be too. I belonged there, not in here with this gargantuan gut bucket. How though? How could I contrive such a transfer? Lorraine wanted me here. Even if I could talk Andy into a job swap, Lorraine would never sanction such a switch. This dilemma required a Machiavellian mind to bring about a positive solution and I knew just the mind.

...

It wasn't easy to get Sweeney's number. Personnel were funny about handing out confidential information like that. Fortunately The Beastmaster was able to offer his services, shagging one of the old boilers that worked in there and obtaining it from her. The number was old; his parents' number from his application form, but it was just possible he had returned to his parents or that they would have a contact number for him.

I picked up the phone and punched in the numbers, praying someone would be in. There was a long period of ringing and I was just cursing my luck and about to slam down the receiver when a voice came on the other end of the phone.

'Hello?' said the gruff sounding voice.

'Hi, I'm after Steve Sweeney. Is this the right number?'

'This is Steve Sweeney. Who's that?'

'Whisky.'

'WHISKY! How you doing mate? How'd you get my number?'

'Hi mate, I got it from personnel, just phoning to check up on how you're doing.'

'I'm great. Just got out the hospital.'

'Why? What's up with you?'

'Nothing, just been on the old drugs trials again. My throat's a bit sore mind. I had to have a tube down it for about six hours a day.'

'Fuck me. Is it really worth it?'

'Too right. I've got a cool two grand being deposited into my bank account this week.'

'Two grand? Fuck me, what you gonna spend it on?'

'I'm off to Australia my son.'

'What you're gonna blow it?'

'No I'm going to get a working holiday visa. I intend to work out there, picking fruit or something.'

'Nice one, when you gonna go?'

'Next January probably, can't stand the thought of another British winter.

The next five minutes of the conversation revolved around Sweeney's plans for working in Oz. The pips went on the phone and I asked him to call me back as I needed some advice. He grumbled something about me not having enough coins for the phone, but duly obliged in ringing back.

'So what you need advice about?' he sounded anxious to hurry the call now that he was paying for it.

'An employee, a woman that I have to work with.'

'What you want to shag her?'

'NO! I want to get away from her. I want to engineer a transfer to The Showboat, but I reckon Lorraine won't have any of it.'

'So you get her to refuse to work with you.'

'How am I gonna manage that?'

'She got a boyfriend?'

'A husband.'

'Perfect, then you have to try it on with her. That way she'll scream sexual harassment and they'll have to move one of you.'

'What if they move her?'

'They are hardly likely to move the complainant, are they?'

'Yeah true, but I'm not really prepared to try it on with this woman. You should see her, she's revolting, a dead ringer for the fucking Honey Monster.'

'You'll have to close your eyes and think of Sugarpuffs.'

'It's not just her looks; that woman's breath smells like an ape's arsehole.'

'Proposition her at arm's length.'

'Not exactly sexual harassment, unless I get up close and personal is it?'

'Whisky, you'll think of something. Just make sure you are the only two around when you do it. That way it's your word against The Honey Monster's. If they can't prove anything outright, they can't sack you.'

'Yeah, cheers for the advice mate.'

'No bother, I'll send you a postcard when I get to Australia.'

'I feel like coming with you.'

'Well you need two grand to get a working holiday visa for Australia mate. You got two grand?'

'No.'

'Didn't think so. I'll just send you that postcard.'

'Cheers, see you.'

'Yeah, see you mate. Oh and Whisky, Whisky!'

'Go on, I'm still here.'

'I want my honey!!'

'Yeah, see you, funny bastard.'

'See you.'

Sweeney was right, but how could I try it on with Diane without actually having to touch her or smell her? Asking her for a date wasn't enough. She might take that as a compliment, or worse, say yes. What I needed was shock and awe tactics, really put the wind up the old boiler.

...

105

I was still contemplating this two days later, as I was busy frying fish and battering sausages, when it hit me. An ingenious idea that would have me on my way to The Showboat in no time. I looked through into the shop where Diane was leaning against her counter, greedily consuming a handful of French fries. Richard was over at Lorraine's office and was unlikely to be back for another half hour or so. The timing was perfect. It had to be now.

'Just popping next door for a second,' I shouted to Diane.

'OK love.'

I left the store and entered Everydays supermarket next door. Picking up a copy of The Sun I made my way to the counter to pay. I then returned to Bogart's and went into the stock room at the rear. Opening up the newspaper to page three I found Angela, twenty-two from Surrey popping out at me. Black hair, dark Mediterranean eyes, huge breasts. You'll do, Angela, you'll do.

I began massaging my balls and stroking the head of my cock, steadily obtaining an erection, as I ogled Angela's magnificent breasts. When I was up to full stretch I threw the newspaper into the corner of the room and pulled my hard on out of the zip in my chef's pants.

'Diane!'

'Yes love?'

'I need your help. I can't find the sausages. Can you come and help me?'

'Coming! But I'll warn you, I don't even know what sort of packs they come in.'

'Don't worry you'll know when you find it,' I shouted, throwing my apron onto the fridge and making sure my tunic was tucked in so that it didn't cover my erection.

'Right,' said Diane, entering the room, 'where should I start looking?'

'There's bound to be at least one round here somewhere,' I replied, standing with my hands on my hips, my legs apart like Peter Pan.

'Aren't they normally kept in the chest freezer?' she asked, seemingly oblivious to my cock, which was already beginning to subside at the sight of her.

'Normally yes, but I couldn't find any in there.'

'Well I'm not the best person to ask. I lost my glasses last week and I'm blind as a baby bat without them.'

Great, just fucking great. Now I was going to be forced to make physical contact with the fat fuck. Every fibre of my being was screaming ABORT! ABORT! IT'S A SUICIDE MISSION, but I had come too far.

'Let me look with you,' I said, sidling up to her.

The cloud of halitosis grew thicker as I approached its epicentre and I found myself wishing that I had a moustache, as it might filter out some of the stench. I quickly reassessed the situation and decided against a close encounter of the touching kind.

'What does the package look like?' she asked.

'It's a white box, grab that white box at the bottom of the freezer will you, I think that might be them.'

As she leaned over the freezer she put her hands on the edge to steady herself. Now, I thought, now. I moved to the other side of the freezer, so that I was facing her, and rested my, now flaccid, cock and balls on the freezer's edge.

'Oh here's one,' I exclaimed, resuming the Peter Pan position, and accompanying it with a huge grin and wink.

'Wher...AAGGGHHRRR!!'

Chapter 27

Another day, another trip to Lorraine's office. Still she had been remarkably restrained for some strange reason. I think she may have actually believed my bullshit story about Dianne being somewhat senile. After all, why would a fetching young stud like me want to sexually harass someone as monstrous as Dianne? It didn't add up, but something had to be done. They couldn't ignore an accusation like this and within two days I was transferred to The Showboat.

I loved the bloody place. Day shifts, glorious day shifts. But day shifts mean nights off, and nights off require money, which was one commodity that was now in short supply. Working away from a till had stripped me of a large portion of my disposable income. My cook's wage wouldn't cover more than a couple of good nights out, not when you factored in the exorbitant cost of drugs on camp.

I needed overtime really, but was unwilling to spend any longer slaving in a scorching kitchen, than I was contractually obliged to. I toyed with the idea of glass collecting, as a semi legitimate form of minesweeping like Andy used to on his night off, but didn't like the idea of doing it for six hours at a time. I knew that as the night went on and I became more pissed, I would be increasingly likely to get caught and sacked for being drunk on duty. In the end it was The Beastmaster that gave me the solution to the cash flow dilemma.

'Why don't you do some overtime at the photo shop?' he asked.

'Doing what? Working the counter?'

'Nah man. In the costumes, like I do. Peter got the sack today and they need a replacement to do a couple of hours a night.'

'What did he get the sack for?'

'Fighting.'

'Who with?'

'A customer. Apparently the customer mistook him for a bird in his costume and felt his arse up.'

'What, he was fighting in costume?'

'Yep.'

'What was he dressed as?'

'Postman Pat.'

'Did Sharon take any photo's? You know, of the fight.'

'Nah man, she was too shocked.'

'Now that's a photo I would pay for. Postman Pat brawling with a pissed up customer.'

'It was a bizarre sight mate, like watching Mickey Mouse turn rabid and savaging someone.'

'Well I wouldn't mind the job, but I don't fancy that fucking skin tight Power Ranger suit. Not with my chicken legs.'

'Don't you worry about that pal. That Power Ranger suit is mine.'

...

It wasn't a bad number really. It got hot, real hot, but it was a justifiable way to enter venues and minesweep a few drinks. I quickly learned that the best place to find any leftovers was on top of the various fruit machines around camp. We would work every major venue on camp and this meant my pickings were quite rich.

I preferred wearing the larger costumes, like the Pink Panther and Postman Pat ones. The main reason for this is that they didn't show off my mal-nourished legs, which had started to resemble the type of legs you would see hanging from a crow's nest. There were, however a few downsides to these costumes. The worst one being that the act of urinating became very tricky, especially after a few minesweept pints.

It was also difficult to have a sneaky cigarette in costume. Consequently I spent large amounts of time in toilet cubicles, smoking and struggling to remove the costume to have a piss.

After a couple of shifts I'd got this problem licked. I only smoked while pissing or shitting in the bog, which halved the amount of time I spent in there. Let me tell you now that when you exit a toilet cubicle, dressed as The Pink Panther, leaving behind an almighty stench and wafting away a cloud of smoke you get a few funny looks from the other patrons believe me.

Sharon, the photographer was pretty cool. She was petite, about five foot four and slim, long auburn hair and drowsy looking brown eyes. She had been doing the job all summer and enjoyed it, but hated her supervisor Rob. The story sounded familiar; he had been really nice to her at first, asking her out on a date when she was new, and she'd said yes. After sleeping with her a few times, his attentions wandered elsewhere, namely another new starter. She had asked for a transfer, but there was nothing available at the time, and so she'd stuck it out in the photo shop while applying for various jobs on cruise ships. The good news for Sharon was that she had landed a job, as a photographer on board a Carnival Cruises ship. She was leaving in a week to spend a month with her family back in Nottingham, before flying off to Miami, to spend all winter in the Caribbean.

'I bet you'll be glad to see the back of Rob, then?' I asked.

'Too right, I thought about just walking out when I found out I'd got the job, but to be honest I think he'd like that. He didn't even try to hide his joy, when I told him I was leaving. The funny thing is that when we split, I made an attempt to keep things amicable, be professional, but he just ignored me. It was like I wasn't even there. He's the one that went off with someone else, but he treats me with contempt,

as though I'm the one that's done something wrong.
Bastard.'

'Well, you're the one that's laughing now,' I told her. 'I bet
he'd give his left testicle to be working in the Caribbean
instead of this shit hole.'

'Yeah, I guess, but I'd still like to get back at him
somehow.'

I wanted to help Sharon. I felt sorry for her, guilty even.
That was the way I had treated many a new starter before I
had met Rachael. It's what I'd been planning for Stacey,
when I was her supervisor in Bogart's, had I gotten the
chance. Get them while they're new, before anyone else
does, that was the idea. They often arrived on camp alone,
first time away from home and eager to meet friends. A
friendly invite from the supervisor, especially if he was well
known, with lots of mates was a compliment they would
seldom turn down. A supervisor without any morals was a
formidable predator around camp and I should know, I'd
had the STD's to prove it. So, no doubt, had the vast
majority of our prey. I was glad to be out of that game, glad
to be a minion again. I had been a fairly moral person before
I came here, before I was corrupted by this fucking place.

'Maybe there's a way we could get back at him, before you
leave camp.'

'How?'

'Don't worry, I'll think of something.'

Chapter 28

On Sharon's penultimate shift, I chose the Postman Pat costume. I liked it better than the Pink Panther because quite frankly I don't like wearing pink. That is not to say that I did like wearing a giant foam postman outfit, I just didn't dislike it as much as the bloody pink one.

We set of on our rounds as we had done for the past five days, starting at The Broadway. There was a fair amount of people in there, considering it was so late in the season and the dance floor was heavily occupied. Black Lace were on stage, performing *Superman*, and we watched in horror and amusement as hundreds of customers performed the moves.

> *Sleep.*
> *Wave your hands.*
> *Hitch a ride.*
> *Sneeze.*
> *Go for a walk.*
> *Let's see you swim.*
> *And ski.*
> *Spray.*
> *Macho man.*
> *Sound your horn.*
> *And ring the bell.*
> *OK. Kiss.*
> *Comb your hair.*
> *Wave.*
> *Wave your hands.*
> *Superman!!!*

When the song finished and everyone left the dance floor we got down to business. Sharon took about a hundred pictures, mainly with me and an array of kids, but she also took a number of pictures of redcoats with adult customers.

It was mainly middle-aged men with female redcoats, looking for an excuse to put their arm around a lithe young body. No doubt these pictures were great sellers. I could imagine the fat, balding old fuckers showing the picture to their mates back home, telling them that she was gagging for it or something of the sort.

After an hour, and three half pints, in The Broadway we moved on to The Castle, where the Karaoke contest was in full swing. A group of six girls were up on the stage, singing Madonna's *Like a Virgin*. These girls looked anything but virginal, dressed in skimpy outfits and gyrating against each other in an erotic way as they screeched out the words to the song. What they lacked in musical talent, they more than made up for in sexuality and would no doubt get a large proportion of the male vote, not least because the winner of the competition was obliged to get up and perform again.

We got through a couple more rolls of film, and I got through an unattended pint of cider, before we headed over to Rick's Place. Once again, we were treated to entertainment of the most dubious calibre, in the form of a house band. The band was currently performing a dodgy rendition of Tina Turner's *Simply the Best*. I watched, through the eyeholes of the costume, in horror as the female singer from the band attempted to do the stupid, crab-like sideward dance, that Tina Turner does. God have mercy, I thought. Time for a smoke.

'Just going for a cig, Sharon.'

'OK Whisk, I'll just take some photo's of the band.'

Sitting in the bog, Postman Pat's foam head on my lap, puffing on the Mayfair, and listening to a crap version of *Nut Bush City Limits*, I decided that I would probably try it on with Sharon tonight. I wasn't working for the photo shop the next day and this was the last chance I'd get before she left. I knew exactly when I would do it too. I'd wait until after we finished work and after we had put my plan to stitch

Rob up into action. I was fairly sure my attentions would be well received; Sharon was constantly playing with her hair whenever she spoke to me and was extremely tactile, touching me frequently and stroking my back, she wanted it.

When we finished our rounds we made our way back to the photo shop, where The Beastmaster was waiting for us. The shop was closed so Sharon unlocked the door and we all entered. She led us into the backroom, where all the costumes were kept and switched the light on.

The Beastmaster put on a Spiderman outfit and Sharon put on a Betty Boop costume, I picked up the camera and familiarised myself with the controls while they changed.

'Right, if you get on your knees Sharon,' I said, motioning her in front of The Beastmaster. 'Throw your head back Beastmaster, as though you're in the throws of ecstasy...That's it...Now, Sharon, try to position your hand to look like you're tossing his cock into your mouth and the other as though you are massaging his balls while you are doing it...perfect.'

'Why don't we just do it properly, instead of faking the photo's?' The Beastmaster asked, a cheeky looking grin on his face.

'I'm sure Sharon doesn't want that great bloody thing in her mouth mate. Besides even you'd have a job on reaching all the way into that huge Betty Boop head.'

'So it's true what they say about you is it? I thought you were stuffing socks down your Spiderman tights,' Sharon laughed, poking her head of the foam head.

'Let's just say that if you see a woman on camp in a wheel chair, she isn't necessarily crippled,' The Beastmaster replied, cupping as much of his package in his hand as would fit.

After that photo, we faked a Power Ranger nailing Wonder Woman, Snoopy back-scuttling the Pink Panther and Superman interfering with himself. For the final picture we set the timer and had myself as Zorro and The Beastmaster as Bart Simpson, spit roasting Catwoman while playing cards on her back. I was at the mouth end and could feel myself becoming excited at the proximity of Sharon's mouth to my genitals. I'm definitely going to make a move later, I thought.

When we finished shooting the pictures Sharon went into the darkroom and started work on developing them. I began packing away the costumes and giggled to myself as I imagined what Rob's face would look like when he realised what had been done. When the pictures were developed we started pulling down random photos from the walls of the shop and replacing them with our own.

The beauty of the plan was that the pictures would probably be spotted by a customer, browsing through, looking for a picture of themselves. This would no doubt cause a serious complaint, after which Rob, as the supervisor, would be forced to scrutinise every wall of the shop looking for other pornographic images. Also, because we were in costumes they would be pretty hard to spot among the genuine photographs, it would take at least an hour to make sure he had removed them all. The costumes provided anonymity for The Beastmaster and I. Of course we would be suspects, as we worked for the shop, but nothing could be proved and Sharon swore not to reveal our identities.

As I packed away the last of the outfits into the box, I thought of what I was going to say to Sharon. 'Fancy going for a drink?' seemed to be the sensible option. That way if she turned me down I was only asking to go for a drink. I'd never had the balls to ask girls out properly, not when sober anyway, and I reflected on the fact that maybe this was why I drank. I did like getting pissed, but preferred getting laid and that only seemed to happen when I lost my inhibitions. The few leftover drinks I'd consumed had all but worn off by now. I'd ask her for a drink, get us both half pissed and then try it on. Taking a deep breath, I stood up straight and marched into the darkroom. Coming from the light as I did so I was completely blind when I entered but I thought I could hear giggles as I went inside.

'Sharon?'

'Er, don't come in, I won't be a minute.'

'I just want to talk to you.'

'Look Whisky,' I heard the gruff voice of The Beastmaster, 'we're kind of in the middle of something here.'

As my eyes adjusted I could just make out the silhouette of The Beastmaster leaning back against the wall, while Sharon was on her knees, in almost the exact pose she had been in her Betty Boop outfit. Only this time there was no faking, she really did have his cock in her mouth.

Chapter 29

I was in a pretty bad mood the next day at work. I had been forced to listen to Sharon's screaming all night as The Beastmaster impaled her not once but three times. She clearly had a night to remember and through the paper thin walls I could hear her informing him of this frequently.

'Fucking hell,' she'd exclaimed, 'I'm gonna need to take a picture of that thing, as a souvenir.'

'Be my guest love, as long as you take one of it in your mouth. Give me a souvenir at the same time.'

'Let me go get the camera.'

After that I'd finally managed to doze off, about two hours before I was due to start work. When my alarm went off, I got up and dug out the cleanest, dirty shirt I could find from my laundry box. It smelled of a mixture of sweat and deodorant, so I gave it an extra coat of deodorant, liberally applying it in the region of the armpits. I decided to skip breakfast and have a ten minute power nap, fully dressed of course. The alarm went off again and I jumped up, went to the bathroom and brushed my teeth. As I brushed away I noted how worn the bristles were on the brush and wondered when I had purchased this dilapidated old item. Had it even been this season? Possibly not, it looked so old. I made a mental note to procure a new one and set off to work.

The Showboat was almost opposite the photo-shop and I felt a twinge of guilt as I passed the front of the store. No doubt at some point today I would be forced to defend myself against accusations of wrongdoing.

I entered the kitchen from the side door and said hi to the supervisor, Sian.

'Hi Whisky,' she replied. 'Listen, before you get changed, would you do me a favour?'

'Sure, what?'

'Brian hasn't shown up to open the bar at The Gaiety Theatre. Lorraine wants someone to go wake him up. Would you go give him a knock? He's probably slept in, he was on a late shift last night.'

'Yeah, course. He's in K16 isn't he?'

'Let me just check...Yes, K16...Cheers Whisk.'

So Barely Breathing Brian was late for work was he? Silly old bastard. Still, that suited me, got me out of the roasting environment of the kitchen for a few extra minutes. I could chain smoke a couple of cigs as I wandered over too.

K16 was a supervisor's chalet, that Barely Breathing Brian had all to himself. I approached the door and began hammering away. No answer. I knocked on both bedroom windows and still received no reply. Hmm, odd, maybe the old bastard had walked out. After twenty odd years of service, maybe he'd finally had enough and shot through. I headed for the accommodation office and knocked on their door.

'Come in,' came a voice from inside.

'Hiya,' I greeted the skinny, bald bloke that sat behind the desk. 'I've been sent to knock on Brian Cunningham, in K16 and there's no answer. Do you think you could open his chalet, to see if he's there? I reckon he's shot through.'

'What, Brian? Never, he'll be here long after you've gone mate.'

'Well he ain't answering his door. Could you come and check on him with me?'

'Hold on, let me just lock this place up,' he said, lifting his puny body out of his chair.

We headed over the chalet and knocked again. No answer. Turning the key in the door, the accommodation manager shouted.

'Brian...It's Gary, from accommodation...You in here?'

No answer. We made our way into the living room, which still had all Brian's possessions lying around, so I guessed he hadn't done one. The first bedroom was empty, not even a bed, there was no point, Brian hadn't had a roommate in years. I always thought he liked it that way. The second bedroom, Brian's was a right old mess, like Dale's had been. It stank of, piss and sweat but there was another smell too, not too strong and certainly not familiar but very, very unpleasant.

'What's that fucking smell?' I asked.

Gary seemed to know. I could tell by his face that he'd come across this before, and I knew just by looking at him what it was too.

'Check the bathroom!' he ordered.

I went toward the bathroom, half excited, half terrified. I expected to find Brian dead on the bog, Elvis style. The smell was getting stronger. He was definitely in here. The poor bastard must have died taking a shit.

Fuck, the sight that hit me blew away all excitement, leaving only the cold, hard reality of death. Brian was in the bath, which was full of blood. A razor sat on the side, also in a small pool of blood. The hot water tap was still running and was burning, almost melting his left foot, no doubt causing that horrible smell, which reminded me of raw meat.

'Shit, he's…he's in here,' I managed to say, before passing out.

Chapter 30

The police questioning was the thing that I found hardest to deal with. I had played no part in Brian's death, yet couldn't help but look guilty throughout the whole process. I guess I've just got a guilty personality. I was sure that when they had finished asking questions about Brian, their next line of enquiry would be, 'Oh, and do you know anything about some pornographic images that have been planted on the walls of the photo shop?'

I didn't have to answer any questions about the photo shop, to the police or to Butlins. I guess, if I was a suspect in the peculiar case of the pornographic pictures, they thought better of accusing me after my grisly discovery.

The management saw fit to give me the rest of the day off work and a couple more days if I needed them, with pay. Counselling would probably have been a sensible idea, but as it was I counselled myself the only way I knew how, I went out and I got pissed.

...

Scary was due to be working that night but he came to sit with me and he sipped a coke as I knocked back the booze.

'Tell you what's the most fucked up mate. That guy was the first person ever to give me the time of day on this fucking holiday camp,' I informed him. 'When I got here it was mid-season and everyone had their own little gangs already, but that guy he took time to talk to me, you know.'

'Yeah, he was a good guy man, I wish I'd taken the time to get to know him better,' he replied.

'Twenty seven years. He was working here before I was even born, can you believe that?'

'It's a long time.'

'It's a fucking life sentence. The guy was like a prisoner. You hear about prisoners becoming institutionalised. Do you reckon it's possible here?'

'More than possible, probable. This place has a lot in common with a prison, when you think about it. We get fed slop and housed in what is little more than a cell. We work a full week for peanuts. We've got the short-term guys that just do one season and the lifers like Brian. We've even got the fucking inmates committing suicide.'

Scary neglected to mention the more obvious comparison, the fact that like a prison the place was full of criminals.

'So what are you?' I asked. 'Another lifer? Like Brian?'

'Nah, Whisk. I've had enough. This shit today, it's made me realise what a fucked up place this is. That's where it all ends if you don't get out and stay out. You see them leave, every year, and just like prisoners they always give it the same lines, saying that they're done, not coming in here again, blah blah blah. But sure enough you'll see them next season, or failing that the season after. They always come back.'

'Why? Why keep coming back?'

'Because life on the outside is shit if you don't have any money or skills. I mean, how much can you possibly save in a full season here? A grand? And that's if you lived like a monk, staying in every night. That's why they come back, because here everything is done for you. You don't need to worry about the electric or the gas. You don't have to pay rent, council tax or water rates. Shit, you don't even need a television licence. In the real world you need money. Most of the guys that leave here go back to their parents, because they don't have the savings to get their own place. Once you've lived here, in this hedonistic environment, you ain't gonna be too happy living with mum and dad are you? So you come back, saying just one more season and the cycle starts again.'

'Is that what you do?'

'Yep, but not this time. In tunnelling out mate. The great fucking escape.'

'What you talking about?'

'I'm serious, I'm off, and I'm never coming back.'

'Off where?'

'Australia. Maybe look Sweeney up.'

'Keep dreaming mate. Where you gonna get two grand from?'

'I'm gonna nick it.'

'You gonna rob a bank are you?'

'No, I'm gonna rob this place.'

'Stop talking shit will you.'

'I'm not talking shit, I'm serious. Let me ask you a question, and I want an honest answer, OK?'

'OK.'

'Have you ever stolen from Butlins?'

I felt myself blush. I had never told Scary about my various scams, and I didn't want to start now. The paranoiac in me even wondered as to whether he was trying to stitch me up here. Was he an informer?

'No,' I lied.

'Well I have,' he announced. 'I have been fleecing this place, on a very small scale since I arrived here. Don't get me wrong, I don't consider myself to be a thief, but I do believe that this place owes me a little more than seventy quid a week for six day's graft. What I do is supplement my inadequate earnings with a little extra from my till. I have every admiration for the few honest souls left on camp, like yourself, but personally every time I skim from that till I feel I'm taking the power back and that helps me control the anger I feel at being exploited by this money making machine.'

'So you've managed to save two grand?'

'No, I've managed to blow each and every penny on speed, beer and dope.'

'So how you gonna get to Australia, rob the cashier's office?'

'No I'm gonna rob my till.'

'Scary, there's only five weeks left of the season. That's four hundred quid a week, I think they would notice that kind of a drop in sales.'

'Who said anything about skimming? I'm gonna do the big legs with a nights takings.'

'What?'

'You remember those two guys who disappeared from Mr B's last year with the money from the till?'

'Yeah, they went on their break and never came back. But didn't they get caught?'

'Yep, but not charged. When the police found them, they didn't have any money on them. They couldn't prove fuck all. I mean imagine you are the supervisor of Mr B's and a couple of stoners take off one night. You could easily rob the till yourself and claim it must have been the two walkouts. The police have to take all these possibilities into account. If they don't find a smoking gun, i.e. the cash, they can't actually prove anything.'

'So you're just gonna walk out with the money from the till? Then what? Hope you don't get picked up by the police in Skegness with the money still on you? They'd soon notice you weren't coming back from your break you know. You'd be reported to the police within the hour, especially since that trick's already been pulled before.'

'That's where you come in.'

'Me? What can I do?'

'Like you say, they'll soon come looking for me, and they'll no doubt get me before I get on a train. So I need to get rid of the money fast. Hide it, close to camp, where you can pick it up later and post it to me.'

'What and you'd trust me to post it to you.'

'You would if there was two grand in it for you.'

'How much you planning to nick? There can't be anymore than about fifteen hundred quid in your till.'

'I'm planning to nick a grand.'

'What and give me two grand for posting you one?'

'We'll invest the grand.'

'In what?'

'Drugs.'

The plan was simple, beautifully so. Because Scary worked his venue all by himself he relied on staff from The Moonshiner to cover his break. When he took his break, he would phone over, so that the supervisor could send over someone to cover him. While he was waiting for his cover to arrive he would pocket a grand from the till's takings.

He would have to take his break late, so that the till would have more cash in it, then quickly make his way off camp, via the busy main entrance and bury the cash at a pre-arranged point, probably on the caravan park next door to Butlins. Scary would then return to camp, quickly pack his belongings and leave camp again, via the staff entrance, where he would no doubt be noticed going for the bus. He'd quite probably be picked up within the hour, but would have nothing on him whatsoever.

'So how do we turn one grand into four?' I asked.

'Like I said, drugs. In four weeks the 18-30's reunion comes to camp. Do you remember what the police were like last year?'

'Yeah, they had sniffer dogs checking every bus.'

'Exactly, there was a major shortage remember. It wasn't so bad for us, we still had our speed, but the holidaymakers were fucked. We could have made a killing if we'd got enough speed or pills to knock out to them.'

'Yeah, but what about the sniffer dogs?'

'What sniffer dogs? They are only here when the weekend begins. There ain't no fucking dogs mid-week while everything on camp is closed.'

'You clever fucker. What do you think we should knock out?'

'Speed. It's simpler that way. Back in Reading I can buy four hundred grams of speed for about a grand.'

'So how we supposed to knock out four hundred wraps of speed? Especially if you're off camp and I'm working.'

'Well I'll just have to make sure I'm back on camp somehow. We'll also need to enlist the help of your lady friend, Rachael.'

'I'm not so sure I'm her favourite person at the moment mate.'

'Well you better make it up to her. She's a rep right? The punters will probably be coming up to her asking if she knows where they can score. That's what half the 18-30's punters in Ibiza ask their reps. I'll be on camp that week, don't you worry about that. If Rachael and any of her rep mates point the punters in the right direction I'll easily knock out four hundred wraps. Of course I'll get some pills too, and give them to Rachael and her mates for helping us out.'

'Like I said though mate, I'm in the doghouse with Rachael.'

'Well you better start sweetening her up...watch out here comes The Beastmaster. I better get off anyway, I've got work in an hour, don't want to get sacked before the big day.'

'What big day?' asked The Beastmaster, plonking himself on a chair next to me.

'Nothing,' Scary replied. 'Just looking forward to the weekend breaks. Anyway I was just leaving, what brings you here so early anyway?'

'Well, when someone told me that a skinny, old man with yellow teeth and a small shrivelled dick had been found dead in his bathtub, I immediately became concerned about my old pal Whisky. But here he is safe and sound. Thank god, he owes me a tenner.'

'Fuck off you heartless cunt,' I snapped.

'I'm off,' said Scary.

'See you Scary. Sorry Whisky mate. What you drinking?'

'Export.'

'Fancy a chaser?'

'A speed bomb would be nice.'

'I'll go wrap you one up.'

Chapter 31

Scary was a good guy. That's why I went straight to him after I finished with the police, he was a good listener. The Beastmaster on the other hand was a selfish cunt, but he did have his uses. His wisdom was questionable, 'Get yourself laid mate, that'll take your mind off it', but he was usually in possession of narcotics and always in possession of a good sense of humour. On top of that, I did need a good shag and you knew that there was some hope of a shag when he was out with you. The quality of the women would no doubt be dubious, but in the barren desert, that was my sex life, even a cup of luke warm piss would go some way to quenching my raging thirst.

There was a popular misconception among our circle of friends that The Beastmaster only ever shagged women that weighed more than a regular set of bathroom scales could register. This is actually untrue, as he proved in the case of Sharon, he does actually get some nice looking women. He can be likened to an alcoholic, in that he would much prefer to down a bottle of fine wine, or a single malt whisky, but if circumstances obstruct this, he'd rather resort to knocking back a bottle of old spice than having nothing at all. Nothing unusual here really, we've all lowered our standards as the clock ticks closer to closing time, but what really gave him his title of The Beastmaster was the fact that he was so proud of his conquests, all of them. The man quite simply had no shame.

That was why I let him do the groundwork. Without shame, rejection is inconsequential. For me a rapid series of rejections would be immensely damaging to my fragile self-confidence, but The Beastmaster was a remorseless pulling machine. He would not stop until someone, anyone, though preferably female, opened their legs to him. We made our way from pub to pub, The Beastmaster unflinching in his efforts to get our legs up, but without even the slightest sniff of success.

Eventually we ended up in The Broadway. Neil Sedaka had been on earlier, but we'd missed him, thank god. It was still pretty busy though and the dance floor was full of a middle-aged women dancing to an Abba record.

'There's two,' The Beastmaster shouted above the music, as he pointed to a couple of women in the middle of the dance floor. They were well in their forties, and more than a little on the large side.

'Jesus mate, they're old enough to be our mothers.'

'Women don't hit their sexual peak until they're in their thirties.'

'They're well past their thirties.'

'So. Experience mate. I bet they've seen some cock in their time.'

'Yeah, riddled with pox probably and with fannies like a clown's pocket.'

'Chill out mate, just cover the old boy up, I've got a couple of jonnies in my wallet. Extra large mind,' he said holding the crotch of his jeans, as he danced his way in the direction of the two women. I watched him from afar as he whispered into one of the women's ears. She threw her head back and laughed at whatever it was he said. He looked a little upset for a second, before regrouping and whispering something else into her ear. This made her laugh too, but she looked in the direction of his crotch when she did so.

He nodded, smiling, as though he were inviting her to do something. She put her cigarette in her mouth, wincing her eyes as she did so and cupped her hand on The Beastmaster's groin. Her eyes widened in wonder and the end of her cigarette reddened. She then removed the cig from her mouth and I lip-read the words, 'Fucking hell' as she spewed out a cloud of blue-grey smoke.

The second hag had a good grope of The Beastmaster's crotch and the three of them danced around provocatively to the Abba record, causing the dancefloor to empty somewhat as they did so. When the song ended they all came over to join me at a table I had found.

'This here's Whisky, my room mate. Whisky this is Alice and Sarah, they're on holiday until tomorrow!'

'Hi ladies,' I said.

'Hiya,' they cawed at me rather wearily, before turning to The Beastmaster. 'You gonna buy us that drink then are you?'

'Yeah, what you want?'

'Two halves of snakebite and black,' said the uglier of the two, Alice.

We sat in silence as The Beastmaster went to the bar and got in a round of drinks. I sipped my beer, watching the dance floor, in an attempt to avoid having to communicate with the two hags. They didn't talk either, as they were busy touching up their lipstick, which already seemed to be grossly over applied.

...

A couple of hours and several pints later, we decided to get a couple of bottles from Everydays and carry on drinking at the chalet. That way, I secretly reasoned we wouldn't be seen with these two old boilers. I tried desperately to steer us to their chalet, but they insisted on coming back to ours. They said they wanted to see what staff accommodation was like but I had the distinct impression they had kids asleep in bed back at their shed. The Beastmaster was well up for these two, he preferred holiday makers and especially ones on their last night on camp. That way he would be less likely to ever bump into them again, 'I'm not interested in a re-match' was one of his favourite quotes. It was a pugilistic image that somehow seemed appropriate to two bruisers we were currently in tow with.

I led the way back to the shed, trying to maintain a reasonable distance between myself and the slags. I had no wish to be spotted by anyone I knew taking these broad shouldered bertha's back to my room.

'Tell you what mate, you three choose the booze while I go ahead and have a bit of a tidy round as we've got visitors,' I suggested, in a desperate attempt at disassociation.

'Yeah fair enough, stump up some cash for the booze then,' The Beastmaster replied.

I passed him my last tenner and jogged ahead to the chalet. When I got home, I closed all the curtains and put some music on, loud. I choose The Beatles, reasoning that, at their age, these two were unlikely to be into house or techno. When they arrived back, rather loudly, I hurried them indoors and looked around outside to check whether they had been spotted. It appeared not. Rubbing my hands together I asked.

'What you get from the supermarket?'

'A bottle of Taboo, and a bottle of Mad Dog 20/20, orange flavour,' said Alice.

'I let the girls choose,' The Beastmaster said quickly, before I rebuked him.

...

It wasn't the most romantic of scenes, I have to say. The Beastmaster definitely had the pick of the two, who both appeared only too eager to get to grips with his monstrous manhood. They laughed at all his shit jokes, while I sat on the fringes wondering which of the two I would be left with. He finally made his move when *Come Together* came on the stereo, pouncing on Alice, who had just begun stroking his leg after pissing herself at yet another one of his witticisms.

Sarah looked disappointedly at me, her booby prize. We'd hardly said a word to each other all night yet now found ourselves in a position where we had to in order to avoid the embarrassment of watching these two getting it on.

We spoke awkwardly for a few minutes about The Beatles, before she excused herself to go to the toilet. The Beastmaster and Alice made no attempt to separate themselves while I sat there alone. She had her back to me with her tongue down his throat. He opened his eyes and looked at me, winking, before closing them again. I watched his hand slide expertly from her tit to her crotch where he ripped a small hole in her tights. He stuck his hand through the hole and began fingering her while she moaned, kissing his neck passionately.

The track ended and the room was filled with the sound of Alice's slurping on The Beastmaster's neck and the squelching of his fingers slipping in and out of her fanny. Thankfully, after what seemed like an age, the next track began. *I am the Walrus*, how appropriate.

As if sensing my association between the song and the blubbery mammal he was currently fingering, The Beastmaster opened his eyes again while she sucked at the nape of his neck. He shook his head at me while screwing up his face and pointing his eyeballs in Alice's direction. The message was clear, yes she's a disgusting hag, but I'm gonna fuck her anyway. Alice looked up at him to see what he doing and he quickly began kissing her again, while grabbing her hand and yanking it in the direction of his cock.

I got up as she began fumbling into his trousers and went to my room, which faced the bathroom. Leaving my door open I waited for Sarah to reappear.

'I wouldn't go in there,' I said when she eventually came out.

'They busy are they?' she asked.

'Very. Come in here if you want.'

She wanted. I may have been the booby prize, but like me her hopes had diminished as the evening wore on. The process of elimination that is failure and rejection had set two equally unsuccessful souls on a collision course. The only person I was good enough for was her and vice versa. We could either sit and feel sorry for ourselves, or we could fornicate.

We chose the latter. Sarah sat on the bed and, almost sighing, began kissing me while I grabbed at her massive breasts.

'Get your dick out,' she ordered, watching me greedily as I took off my pants. She looked disappointed for a second, then took a hold of my cock and plunged it straight into her mouth. Any reservations I had about Sarah were quickly vanquished as she performed the most amazing blowjob I had ever received. It was the first time I had felt a deep throat performed properly, using the muscles in her throat to massage my penis, and I began to realise why The Beastmaster went for women like this. They did try harder, fuck me, the man was a genius.

The groaning in the other room became louder and I could hear Alice screaming in pleasure.

'Yeah come on you big bastard, fuck me, come on, come on.'

Sarah stood up and yanked up her dress over her head, pulling her knickers to one side. I realised I hadn't got any condoms, but at this moment I didn't particularly care. Whether it was that blowjob or the voyeurism of listening to The Beastmaster blowing Alice's legs off next door, I don't know. Maybe it was the fact that this would be my first shag since I had got back on camp, but at that moment I wanted nothing more than for Sarah to sit her fat, spacious cunt on my dick. She straddled over me and began to lower herself down, I felt the warmth as I entered and she let out a little moan.

'I've changed my mind,' I said pulling out quickly and turning over.

'What? You've changed your mind?'

'Yes, I've changed my mind. I can't do this. I'm still in love with someone else. I'm sorry, I just can't.'

'Never mind someone else. Come here,' she said, attempting to turn me over. 'I'll give you another blowjob, that will get you in the mood.'

'Look,' I said, resisting. 'I don't want a blowjob. I just want you to leave.'

'You fucking skinny little bastard,' she roared. 'You're fucking pathetic. You get me in here and fuck me about like that.'

'GET OUT YOU FAT FUCK! I'M NOT FUCKING INTERESTED!'

Sarah picked up her dress and threw it quickly back on. I didn't turn off my front to watch her leave I just lay there dejected. I could hear her outside ranting on to Alice and The Beastmaster. Then there was a knock on the door.

'Go away you fucking slag. I'm not interested,' I shouted.

'It's me,' said The Beastmaster.

'You can fuck off too. Get them out of our shed, you sick bastard.'

'Bollocks to you,' he replied, moving back into the living room.

I could clearly hear them all talking. Sarah was shouting, while they tried to calm her down. Eventually, the music went back on and after a while I heard the sound of moaning again, three people this time. When I was sure they weren't coming back I turned over from my stomach and looked at the spunk patch I was lying in. I then collapsed back on the bed again, sobbing uncontrollably. I'm still not sure why I cried so much that night. Was it because I had once again cheated on Rachael? Maybe it was finding Brian's body. But then again it might have been the fact that Sarah was the ugliest woman I had ever been with and yet I'd come well before she'd reached the base of my penis.

Chapter 32

Whisky,

I can't believe you, I really can't. I'm sick to death of you going on about Taylor. But if you're so interested in him I'll tell you. We have made up. He's stopped selling drugs and we are friends again, so you can start biting your nails until I get back. I have to say I really did not like the tone of your last letter and if you think calling me a bitch is going to make me respect you more then you are even more stupid than I gave you credit for.

So you've reached the dizzy heights of being a cook in Bogart's have you? What is it they sell there? Oh yes, burgers, chips and fried chicken. Well whoopee bloody doo, now you can apply for a job at Burger King when you finally leave camp (if you ever leave that is).

Incidentally, I do a whole lot bloody more than get pissed and produce stage shows you know. I've told you before how hard the work is, but you only seem capable of hearing what you want to hear. Maybe that's why you are so concerned about me living with a man. You don't seem to have taken in the fact that I don't bloody fancy him!

If you're not going to write anything meaningful, don't bother writing at all.

Rachael.

Chapter 33

Ah, weekend breaks. That double edged sword. Were we cursed or blessed? On the one hand we had half the week off, starting on Monday, which was of course payday. But on the other hand we still had to get in our thirty-nine hours work, over a period of about seventy-two hours.

With so much work to be done in so little time, I personally needed drugs and on previous weekend breaks I'd had a relatively happy time. This season was to be different. I was not operating a till of any description, and would therefore be unable to embezzle any drug/beer tokens. Also, I would be unable to do any overtime for the photo shop, and would miss the extra income this afforded.

Scary had chosen this weekend to jump ship. Cleverly deciding to make his move on the Friday, rather than working the whole weekend for a pay packet he wouldn't be around to collect. He was twitching quite badly, so we were having a few shots of Crème de Menthe to calm him down.

'So what time do you expect to go on your break?' I asked, again.

'I've told you, about nine o' clock,' he replied as his shaking hand lifted his glass to his mouth.

'And you'll bury the money under the generator on the caravan site next door?'

'Yes. Unless anyone's around, in which case I'll bury it next to the petrol station next door.'

'If that place closes at seven, why not just bury it there anyway?'

'I'm more likely to get spotted there, what with it being next to the main road.'

'Fair enough. Good luck mate.'

'Yeah, don't go stitching me up and keeping the money for yourself.'

'What do you take me for?'

'Listen, I've been here for five years. I don't trust no cunt.'

'Yeah well, I wouldn't rip you off mate. Besides I'm looking forward to going to Australia.'

'You got in touch with Rachael yet?'

'I sent her a letter on Tuesday; no doubt it'll be a week or two before she replies. If she replies.'

'She will mate. She loves you.'

'I wish I had your confidence.'

'It'll be cool,' he reiterated before pouring another large glass of the mint liqueur and knocking it quickly back. 'Anyway, I better get off. See you in a couple of weeks.'

'Yeah, see you. Have a good half shift, and don't panic,' I said, closing the door.

'Easy for you to say,' he replied, as he took a deep breath and made his way to the door.

...

When he left I ran the bath as full as it was possible, just deep enough to reach my genitals, and sat in it thinking about what life in Australia would be like. Afterwards I shaved and then I was ready. The seventies weekend beckoned.

The camp was a hive of activity as I wondered over to work. Coaches, cars, caravans and cabs were dropping guests off on camp and large queues of people had formed where the customers collected their keys to the chalets. The majority of the clientele were in their forties and many of them were dressed in glam seventies clothing, like some sort of Gary Glitter convention. Jesus, I thought, The Beastmaster will be in his element with some of these old hags. My mind then began replaying images of my encounter with Sarah and I shuddered as I entered The Showboat, via the kitchen door, to start work.

Chapter 34

My shift ended at two in the morning and I was back up again for work eight hours later at ten. I had hardly slept, wondering how Scary had got on with the plan. I couldn't exactly ask the management or security about him, as this would no doubt implicate me in the theft.

I set my alarm for nine fifty, which just gave me enough time to wash my face and brush my teeth. I had missed breakfast, again, and suppressed my appetite and nerves with two consecutive Mayfairs. I then trudged back to The Showboat, which I would be seeing a lot of over the next couple of days, and pushed open the kitchen door.

'Morning Sian,' I yawned to the team leader.

She looked blurry eyed, not surprisingly as Team Leaders were expected to work forty-five hours over the weekend. 'Morning Whisk. Lorraine told me to send you over to the office.'

'Me? Why?'

'I don't know Whisk, but she wants to see you now.'

'Fair enough,' I said exiting the door.

I had been expecting the call, it was inevitable. They knew that Scary and I went back a long way. I was bound to be questioned as to his whereabouts. I ambulated slowly towards the office, sick off the sight off that place, Lorraine in particular. Pushing open the door I made my presence known to Julie and asked her to inform Lorraine that I was here to see her. Julie gave me a look that made me think of a doctor handing over some bad news, sympathetic, yet clinical, then made her way into Lorraine's office.

'You can go in now,' she said when she re-emerged.

I got up from my seat, inhaled deeply and walked into the room.

'Hi Lorraine,' I said, feigning amiability.

'Sit down Paul.'

'Sounds ominous.'

'Yes I'm afraid it is Paul.'

'Is it about Brian?'

'No. No it's not. It's about Paul Carey.'

'Scary? Is he all right?'

'I was hoping you could tell me Paul. He walked out of work last night and took all his belongings with him.'

'Oh my god, he's left?'

'It would seem so. Have you any idea why he might do this?'

'Well he hasn't been very happy recently, but I never expected him to leave. This is his home, he's been here a good five years.'

'Yes it's very unexpected, I agree, but as you know people leave here all the time.'

'That's right, they do.'

'The problem is, that when Paul Carey left, so did twelve hundred pounds of company money.'

'What?'

'When I went to cash up his till, it was down by twelve hundred pounds.'

Well the old bastard got away with more than he expected, I thought to myself. That extra two hundred quid would go some way to seeing us through a week or so before flying of to Australia.

'Have you tried to contact him? Presumably you have an emergency contact number from his application form,' I asked Lorraine.

'Yes we do, but we've no need to contact him. We noticed he was missing fairly quickly and security caught up with him at the bus stop down the road. I was just wondering if you might have any idea why he would do such a stupid thing.'

'You mean he actually stole it? I'm amazed. I can't believe that Scary is a thief. And to take twelve hundred pounds, that's just crazy.'

'Well people do stupid things sometimes. Speaking of which, I have had some complaints from the management team of the photo shop.'

'Really?'

'Yes, apparently a former member of their staff made some pornographic photographs and put them on display in the shop. The manager seems to think that you might know something about this prank, which would of course be a sacking offence.'

'Nothing to do with me,' I exclaimed, rubbing my nose. 'What gives you the right to implicate me?'

'Now wait a minute Paul. I'm not blaming you. I am merely warning you that you are one suspect in the investigation of a prank that the photo shop are taking very seriously.'

'I'm not happy about that. If he wants to accuse me of something, he should do it to my face. I don't know anything about any photos and I don't know why Paul Carey would go mad and steal twelve hundred pounds,' I shouted. I was starting to believe my own lies and I felt a wave of anger about the injustice of these accusations. Who the fuck did these bastards think they were? I'd had just about enough of this. 'You know I'm sick of being accused of things that I haven't done Lorraine. I can't take much more. I've been demoted already this season and now you seem to be implicating me in everything that goes wrong around camp.'

'You have been in this office a lot recently Paul. Perhaps the time has come for you to think about which direction your career at Butlins is taking.'

Career? Was this bitch talking about Butlins here or what? Wait a minute, what was she insinuating here?

'What do you mean, which direction my career is taking? Are you suggesting that I should leave?'

'I'm not suggesting anything. I am merely noting that you started out the season as a promising young section leader, yet now you work as a cook and dress up as the Pink Panther. Not only that, but your visits to my office are becoming increasingly frequent.'

'Are you going to sack me?'

'No.'

'Of course not. You'd have to go through the disciplinary process first. You'd rather I just left, wouldn't you? Well I'm not going anywhere. I'll be here for a good few years yet.'

'Not necessarily Paul. Don't forget that when the season ends, so does your contract. We don't have to give you a new one for next season, you know. I suggest that if you do want another contract, you keep yourself out of trouble for the next three weeks.'

'Is that everything?'

'Yes, you can leave.'

'Thanks, bye,' I said sarcastically as I left.

I slammed the door and stormed back to work, apoplectic with rage about the accusations. Outside the kitchen I sparked up a Mayfair and tried to calm myself down. It seemed to do the trick, so I lit another from the stub of the first and started to laugh. Fuck me, was I mad? Everything I had been accused of was true, why was I so incensed? I'd done it all, and more, yet the feeling of injustice had been real, I wasn't acting.

Huh, Scary had been caught eh? I wondered if he had managed to bury the cash first, or had he been caught with it? If he had been caught with the cash, had he told the police about my involvement? Would it be safe to even attempt to dig it up now, or would the police be waiting to pounce on me? Fuck.

Chapter 35

That shift seemed to last all week. The monumentally important task of frying fish and chips and grilling burgers was completed in something of a haze, as I fretted about what to do when I finished. Would I still look for the money, or were the police lying in wait for me? I knew nothing about the police, only that they were the enemy of petty criminals like myself. Would they pump valuable resources into staking out a few hundred quid? I wasn't sure.

I decided it would be better to leave the money a couple of days. After all, I wouldn't be able to post it until Monday anyway. Yes, that was the best plan, I'd leave it until Monday.

When my shift finally ended, my first stop was the staff club. As I approached I could hear Ultranate's, *You're Free* reverberating around a hollow building. I poked my head inside. There were two people on the dance floor and a handful of chalet monsters drinking at a couple of tables. No doubt everyone was working or exhausted after a thirteen hour shift. I decided to have a quick beer anyway and made my way towards the bar. As I approached it I felt a tap on my shoulder. I turned around to face Knuckles, who had an evil looking grin on his face.

'Saw boyfriend last night,' the cock remarked.

'Oh yeah, who's that then?' I asked.

'Mr Carey.'

'I hope you didn't upset him. He can get violent when he's angry you should know that.'

'Oh I upset him all right. I found him before the police.'

'What you talking about?'

'Well, when your sweetheart went missing along with his till, me and the boys went looking for him around camp. I spotted him just off site at the bus stop and while one of the lads phoned the police, me and two others went to pay him a visit.'

'I suppose you'll get a medal from Des,' I laughed.

'No. But I got the satisfaction of cracking a couple of your boyfriend's ribs.'

'Bullshit.'

'Bullshit eh? Would you like to see what these things do to ribs?' he said, producing what appeared to be a pair of brass knuckles.

I backed away from him, unsure whether he intended to harm me, or was just trying to intimidate me.

'Now you know why they call me Knuckles,' he laughed. 'And believe me, so does your mate.'

'And I suppose the police just let you get away with it did they?'

'The police were just happy that they didn't have to postpone their supper looking for a thief. As far as they are aware, Mr Carey became violent and we were forced to restrain him, they didn't need to know about the knuckle duster.'

'So did they find any money on him? Or is he innocent?'

'As a matter of fact, they didn't find any money on him. But that doesn't mean he didn't have any.'

'What are you saying? If he didn't have any money, he's innocent.'

'I'm saying that carrying around a large amount of money like that would be dangerous. Maybe he got mugged.'

'You mugged him?'

'Maybe.'

'Bollocks, he'd have told the police.'

'Sure, and in doing so, admit that he'd stolen the money. Don't talk shit.'

'I think you're talking shit. I think he didn't even have any money on him, and I think the police will have released him without charge. No money, no crime.'

'Oh the police never even took him to the station. They searched him and then took him to the hospital.'

'What? Is he still there?'

'How would I know? He's your boyfriend not mine. Anyway, I've got work to do, enjoy your beer.'

'Fuck you.'

'Don't get lippy son, there's a few weeks of the season left yet. You wouldn't want to join your mate in the accident ward would you?'

The threat was real. I could see the malevolence in his eyes. There was no way I could beat this fucker, he'd already gotten the better of me once and another fight with him would mean a quick trip to casualty and a swift end to my season. Better to bide my time and figure something out for 18-30's weekend.

Chapter 36

I opened the door to Scary's hospital ward and walked in. I recognised him straight away, yet he looked different in his blue hospital smock, skinnier and paler, apart from the black and blue of his swollen face.

'Was the facelift successful?' I joked, in an attempt to make light of his situation.

'Hello mate,' he mumbled softly, it obviously hurt him to speak, judging by the grimace he made as he did so.

'How are you?' I asked, and immediately cursed myself for asking such a stupid fucking question. How the hell did I think he was? He had a fractured eye socket for god's sake.

'Not too bad. These pain killers are quite trippy.'

'Trust you to be getting off your face, even when you are in hospital,' I replied sitting at his side and holding his hand. He squeezed mine back and tried to smile, but winced and gave up. 'Have your parents been to see you?'

'No man. I don't want to worry them. I'll be out soon, might as well tell them when I get home. No point in them rushing over here.'

'Do you remember what happened to you?'

'Yeah, I remember bits. It was Knuckles. Him and his mates jumped me.'

'What about the police? Have they been to question you?'

'Yeah. They're coming back again. They want to know if I can describe my attackers.'

'What'd you tell them?'

'I told them that I couldn't remember.'

'Why? You should grass the fuckers up. They could have killed you, or blinded you. Plus they nicked your cash.'

'Nicked what?' he said looking alarmed all of a sudden.

'Your cash. The money. They mugged you.'

'How did they know where it was buried?' he asked, struggling to sit up and looking at me accusingly.

'Buried? I thought they mugged you and took it from you.'

'No mate,' he answered, looking a little more relieved. 'I buried it, as we planned. I buried it at the caravan site.'

'So have the police questioned you about the money as well?'

'Yes, but I've told them I can't remember anything. I don't know what cash they're talking about.'

'You clever bastard. So they think the money is long gone, and can't prove your involvement in the theft at all.'

'I love it when a plan comes together.'

'Yeah, all right Hannibal. I'd light you a cigar, but I don't think they allow it in here. Listen do you know how long you're gonna be in here?'

'I'm supposed to get out tomorrow. Why?'

'Well if we're still sticking to the plan, I'll dig up the money and post it to your mother's house tomorrow. That way you'll be there to receive it when it gets there the day after. Then you can get the whiz.'

'Yeah, that sounds good, but I'm not sure I'll be up to coming back on camp to knock that stuff out. Not while Knuckles and his mates are about, and I'm in this condition. Do you think you'll be able to get rid of it?'

'I'll be working. I won't have time.'

'What about Rachael?'

'I told you before mate. We are barely on speaking terms, I can't expect her to start pedalling class A narcotics for me can I?'

'Well you'll have to convince her. Either that or you could blob work and sell it yourself.'

'I can't take a whole weekend on the sick; they'll check my chalet and fire me if I'm not in bed.'

'Well you'll just have to sell it all in one night. It's only four hundred wraps, and there'll be about ten thousand drug hungry punters on camp. It should be easy. Here I'll tell you how we're gonna do this...'

Chapter 37

I left the hospital at five o' clock, when it was starting to get dark. It was pissing it down outside, as usual. I waited at the bus shelter, which rattled with the wind that blew in from the sea. When the bus arrived I jumped aboard, paid my fifty pence fare and watched the monsoon through the windows as we drove past the numerous caravan parks that lined the road from Skegness. Eventually, we passed Butlins and the caravan park next door. I asked the driver to stop about half a mile further down the road. When he did I alighted and pulled my hood up to shield me from the wind and rain, which appeared to be coming down even faster now.

There was zero traffic about and I began to follow the road back towards the caravan park. As I approached the park I heard the sound of a vehicle displacing water from the flooded road behind me. The headlights lit the road ahead of me and the car slowed as it got closer. Why the fuck was the car slowing? I wondered, in a fit of paranoia. Take it easy, probably doesn't want to splash you and soak you as he passes. Be calm, be calm. As the car drew level with me, I looked across at it. Two faces stared back at me, both male and mean looking. The car slowed a little more. I smiled. The passenger stared at me blankly, before the driver sped up again and disappeared into the distance.

...

The caravan park was dead, even quieter than Butlins. Not a single light came from within the caravans and I immediately felt more relaxed, as this lessened my chances of being spotted. I made my way towards the entrance, then followed the path up towards the point where Scary had buried the cash. It was just as he said it would be; three tent pegs had been stuck into the ground to form a triangle.

Casting a glance over each shoulder to make sure I wasn't being watched, I began digging with the two dessert spoons I had stolen from the hospital on my way out.

It was an arduous unearthing, which took a lot longer than I thought it would. Despite the rain, the ground was rock solid and I cursed Carey for his un-necessarily deep excavation. My nerves were getting the better of me and I must have looked like a particularly paranoid gazelle, as I constantly checked over each shoulder, convinced that I would be discovered by some sort of security guard at any moment.

When I eventually exhumed the loot, I almost burst into tears.

'Yes, you fucking dancer,' I screamed, like Renton finding his opium suppositories at the bottom of the bog in *Trainspotting*.

Sticking the booty into my jacket I took another glance over each shoulder, before jogging towards the caravan park's exit. The road was as quiet as it had been an hour before. All I had to do now was get the bloody cash on camp and I was sorted.

...

It was only a five-minute walk back to the staff entrance and I smiled to myself the whole way, despite the lashing rain and the gale force winds. Approaching the entrance to camp I looked cautiously at gate, trying to ascertain who was on duty. There was someone moving around near the window. Whoever it was had a balding head with a smattering of grey hair on the sides. It certainly wasn't Knuckles, so I decided to use this entrance rather than the main one. I approached the barrier, smiling and took out my staff identification as I did so. The whole process of leaving and re-entering camp always reminded me of a cold war movie, with border guards suspiciously eyeing you and your documents, before finally declaring, 'Your papers seem to be in order,' in a dodgy Russian accent.

As I got to the barrier I realised I had blundered. There wasn't one security guard in there, there were three. Shit, and one of them was fucking Knuckles.

'Evening,' I said to the bald guard as he came to the window. I flashed my card and he waved me past. 'Thanks,' I added, making my way past the barrier.

'Hold on a minute,' shouted the familiar voice of Knuckles. 'Where have you been?'

'The hospital, visiting a sick friend.'

'So how come you're covered in mud?' he asked.

'I fell over.'

'Fell over eh? You don't look drunk to me.'

'You don't have to be drunk to fall over do you? It's raining, the grass is slippery. Is falling over a breach of company rules?'

'It just looks a bit strange that's all. You're soaking wet, covered in mud and just came from the opposite direction to the hospital.'

'I caught the bus, but missed my stop.'

'You must have missed it by a long way to get that wet.'

'Well maybe I needed a walk to clear my head after seeing how badly hurt my friend was.'

'Badly hurt is he? That's a shame. Give him my regards next time you see him.'

'You never know, he might give you *his* regards if he ever sees you again,' I quipped.

'On your way Mr. Hisky,' he replied. 'Don't want you to catch pneumonia.'

I could feel his eyes digging into me as I took my leave and headed towards my chalet. About two hundred yards down the path I looked over my shoulder, and there he was, still watching me. I couldn't see his eyes, but knew they were laden with hatred and suspicion.

Chapter 38

'Chalet check!' came the shout as I heard the door being opened. There was then a boisterous knocking at both my room door and The Beastmaster's.

'What the fuck?' I heard The Beastmaster shouting from inside his room.

'Chalet check! Please open your door,' came the reply, it sounded like Knuckles.

'Chalet check? It's fucking four in the morning. What you doing a chalet check at this time for?'

'We have reason to believe that there are drugs in this chalet.'

'Drugs? What drugs?' The Beastmaster sounded a little less cocky now. 'Let us get our clothes on, won't be a minute.'

Us eh? Might have known that bastard would have company. Putting my clothes on I wondered if The Beastmaster had anything on him. No doubt, if he did, he was busy swallowing it right now.

I was first out. There were three security guards in total, Knuckles and his two cronies, Gary and Lee. A couple of minutes later, The Beastmaster came out, accompanied by a male redcoat. He looked pretty red himself. 'Let us put our clothes on,' he had said. He looked at me uncomfortably; this was pretty much the first time I had ever seen him embarrassed. I gaped back in astonishment. This guy would fuck anything.

'Right can you all stand by the wall over here please,' said Knuckles, smirking at The Beastmaster.

We stood at the wall, and watched as two of the security guards systematically inspected our shed. My room was searched first, nothing found. Then the bathroom, nothing found. The Beastmaster's room was next, again nothing. Then came the, so called, living room. I watched The

Beastmaster's face contort in discomfort as they approached our wall clock. The clock face read half past eight. It had read this time for months. Not because it was broken but because where the pencil battery was supposed to be we had instead concealed, what we called, our emergency stash. Two wraps of speed, that we left there in case of...well...emergencies. The Beastmaster grimaced as Knuckles pulled the clock from the wall.

'Looks like this thing needs some new batteries,' he exclaimed as he inspected it.

'No it's just broken I think,' The Beastmaster replied.

'Let's have a look then,' said Knuckles, smiling as The Beastmaster closed his eyes. 'Empty, no wonder it doesn't work.'

The Beastmaster opened his eyes again, and looked at me accusingly. I shrugged, then winked as I nodded towards the redcoat.'

'Fuck you,' The Beastmaster mouthed back.

'Looks like we're done in here boys,' declared Knuckles, heading towards the door, followed by his associates. 'You can get back to your gay orgy if you like.'

With that he slammed the door and I heard the three of them laughing as they walked away.

'You thieving bastard!' The Beastmaster turned to me.

'Well you ungrateful twat, we'd have both been sacked if they had found those wraps.'

'That's no excuse. Those wraps were for the two of us. You better replace them.'

'Don't worry, I'll replace them.'

'I think I'm going to leave,' said the redcoat, Simon, to The Beastmaster. 'Goodnight Craig. Goodnight...er... Whisky, is it?'

'Yes mate, goodnight,' I waited until he'd left before looking at The Beastmaster and pissing myself. 'Let us get our clothes on,' I mimicked.

'Fuck you. What was I supposed to say? Let me just swallow this joint?'

'Yeah, I'm sure you were swallowing something.'

'Look I'm warning you Whisky, shut the fuck up. We were having a smoke, OK? When they came knocking I had to buy myself enough time to get rid of the fucking stuff. That's why I said that.'

'Personally, I'd rather get the sack for the drugs than have Knuckles go around telling everyone that he found me in bed with a male redcoat.'

'Whose he gonna tell?'

'God knows with that vindictive twat. Everyone he talks to I imagine.'

The Beastmaster looked worried, very worried. I had no sympathy for the cunt, after all he wouldn't for me.

Chapter 39

The next morning I didn't mess around. I got up and bought a padded envelope from the post office on camp. I then retrieved the bin bag containing the thousand pounds and two 'emergency' wraps of speed from the rubbish pile at the end of the chalet block, and retired to my shed. Once there I took the money from the bin bag and stuffed it in the padded envelope. It had been a risk leaving the money in the rubbish bag, but a calculated one. I just knew that Knuckles would suspect something and reasoned that it was safer there than in our shed. Hiding the two wraps of whiz was just an added precaution, and one that I was glad I had taken. I then went back to the post office and posted the cash, recorded delivery to Paul Carey.

It was the height of cheek delivering the money from the post office on camp, but I thought it less of a risk then negotiating the security guards at the gate. I knew that to tamper with the post is a very serious offence and that Her Majesty's Royal Mail was by far the safest way of getting anything off camp.

I had counted the money before I put it in the envelope and there was exactly a thousand pounds. Lorraine had told me that Scary had stolen one thousand two hundred. Then it became clear to me. That's why Knuckles had claimed to have relieved Scary of the cash. He had, but only two hundred quid of it. He must have known there was more, that's why he raided my chalet last night. He knew I had the rest.

If Scary had planned to take two hundred quid for himself, how could I trust him not to rip me off with the rest of the money? I toyed with the idea of keeping it all, just in case, but was afraid that it would be discovered over the next few days. Better to take a gamble and post it to Scary. That was the only way I'd get enough money together to haul myself out of this place and over to Australia. But I was biting my nails when I posted the cash, wondering if I'd ever hear from Scary again.

...

A week later, I still hadn't heard from either Carey or Rachael. That bitch was no doubt banging away with that sly fucker Taylor, but where was Carey? He'd ripped me off. I'd taken all those risks and he'd fucking stitched me up. I knew I should have kept that money, you couldn't trust anyone that had been tainted by this place, not one of the fuckers.

Chapter 40

The, so-called, adult weekend seemed to go on forever. It was by far the weakest link in the weekend breaks. The line up for The Showboat consisted of bunch of sleazy comedians; the most famous of which was Bernard Manning and a group of male strippers. I hardly even bothered going out. It was too depressing. The Beastmaster wanted to though. He wanted to watch the male strippers, claiming that the place was 'bound to be full of fanny!' But, after the events of the other night, I was starting to notice another side to The Beastmaster. Why was he obsessed with threesomes? Was he into men and women?

'Why don't you take your mate Simon?' I taunted him, referring to the redcoat.

'Listen, you witless twat, I've told you about that! I'm not fucking gay! All-right?'

'Nobody's saying you're gay, merely that you appreciate both the male and female form.'

'I'm warning you Whisky. You better shut the fuck up about that. I'm not in the mood. It's bad enough with that wanker Knuckles and his lot. I don't need my own mates winding me up as well.'

'Giving you shit is he?'

'I'm telling you mate, he's seriously damaging my reputation. Every time I go in the staff club, him and the other security guards start talking to me in poofter voices. I must have lost about three potential shags this week because of those cunts.'

'Well there's only a week left mate. Maybe you should try a different camp next year, Minehead or Bognor Regis. I'm sure there's an abundance of untapped fanny down there.'

'Full of bloody southerners though aren't they?'

'So. Southerners aren't from another country you know. They do speak English down there.'

'Ah, even so. I was thinking about going over to Pontins, in Blackpool. Supposed to be a fucking magic night out over there like.'

So another one planning to jump ship, I thought, as I watched him getting ready to go watch the male strippers. If Carey didn't turn up with the speed, that would mean that I would be the only one left next season, if they'd even have me. Why, oh why hadn't I saved any money? Another season on camp loomed like a custodial sentence and this one would be without the lads as well as without Rachael. Where was that fucker Carey? Where were those drugs?

When Carey still hadn't been in touch by Thursday night, I knew he'd fucked off and taken the money. I knew because there was no way that he would be able to get the speed on camp the following day. It would be almost impossible. The police and sniffer dogs checked every bus that came on camp. They were also strategically placed around the entrances and the car park. The only thing missing was a German style watchtower. It just wasn't worth the risk. That was why anyone with drugs, any drugs was sure to clean up this weekend.

It was a fitful night, without much sleep, which was a real pisser, because I knew I would be working for the best part of fourteen hours the day after. I also knew that, after work, I would be keen to make something of the liveliest weekend in the Butlins calendar and try to forget about my woes. That would leave me even more exhausted at work the second day, and without the prospect of a chemical pick me up this was a depressing thought indeed.

Chapter 41

So this was it, the legendary 18-30's reunion. The highlight
of our season, which we had waited nine long months for.
Nine long months of Black Lace and house bands. Nine
months of families with screaming brats or groups of old
folks, like the cast from the film *Cocoon*. Nine months of
customers who were the very antithesis of the staff. The staff
were young, highly sexed and, for the most part, off their
tits. In other words, just like 18-30's holiday makers, these
were our kind of customers.

After a full season of shagging fellow members of staff,
and thereby running the risk of falling into a long-term
relationship, the camp workers were free to indulge in guilt
free, pressure free sex. It mattered not if you only lasted
thirty seconds, you would not endure the humiliation of
bumping into these women in the staff canteen. They would
be gone by Monday and with them your dirty little secret.
These were the fabled weekends that we veterans of
previous seasons told tales of to the newcomers. 'Just stick it
out till November', we would tell them. 'Believe me, you
won't regret it.'

I could feel the excitement around me in the staff canteen,
as I pushed my lunch around my plate. The place was
buzzing with anticipation. I on the other hand was one
morose mother fucker. I barely looked up when Sian, my
team leader stood next to my table and asked if she could
join me.

'Yeah, sure,' I mumbled, motioning her down.

'Looking forward to tonight?' she asked.

'Not really.'

'What's up?'

'Nothing, I just couldn't get to sleep last night.'

'Bet you're still going out though.'

'Dunno.'

'Well someone's in a good mood.'

'Sorry,' I sighed. 'Like I said, I didn't get much sleep.'

'Well I don't want to upset you any more than you already are, but Lorraine told me to send you over to her when you get to work.'

'What now?'

'Don't know Whisk. She just asked me to send you over.'

Jesus. Was there no end to Lorraine's antagonism? Why did she wish to make my last weekend even more of a misery? Could I not have three days without the threat of the sack hanging over me? I finished my lunch and trudged over to the office. There was no-one at the reception desk so I went straight to Lorraine's door and knocked loudly.

'Come in,' came an unusually cheerful voice. Oh, god, the woman must have found a reason to sack me if she had a cheerful voice. 'Hi Paul,' she continued, still cheerfully.

'Er, hi Lorraine. You wanted to see me?'

'Well not really to see you, I just asked that you would come over to the office. There's some post here that you still haven't collected and it's the last weekend of the season, so you better take it before you leave.'

'But I've been checking the mail every other day,' I replied.

'You obviously haven't been checking hard enough. There's a letter and a parcel.'

'A parcel?'

'Yes, they're in The Showboat's pigeonhole. Close the door on your way out will you.'

I closed the door all-right. A parcel. Who else would send me a parcel, but Scary Carey? It had to be the drugs. I rummaged through the pigeonhole and dug out the letter, posted from Tenerife and a large padded envelope. I squeezed it; trying to ascertain whether he had been stupid enough to send a bag of speed, without concealing it in something like a teddy bear or a video cassette box. It felt

hard. Must be a video cassette box. The postmark said
London, but Scary was from Nottingham. What did this
mean? Was it from Scary? Maybe he had thought a
Nottingham postmark would alert Lorraine, after all he knew
we picked our mail up from her office.

Clever bastard.

There was no way I was going to open the parcel yet. I was
on a split shift, I could wait until four o' clock. I would leave
the letter until four too. I almost skipped back to work. Scary
had taken a massive gamble, risking my liberty and
livelihood I hasten to add. But I was willing to forgive his
stupidity, as he hadn't ripped me off after all.

God bless the old fucker.

The first part of my shift passed quickly, I was now in the
same jovial mood as everyone else and talked excitedly with
Sian about the Digweed set that was on that night. With the
prospect of a 'speedy' evening shift, I didn't even mind the
fact that I would be working until two in the morning.

At four bells, I finished the first half of my split shift and
grabbed my parcel and letter to take back to my chalet. I
didn't even get out of my chef's whites. I merely threw a
coat over them, I was so eager to open my parcel. Not
fancying any unwanted attention however, I stuffed the
parcel under my coat in case I bumped into The
Beastmaster, or Knuckles and his mates. Opening the door
to my shed, I made sure the place was empty, before digging
the parcel out and ripping it open. Inside the packaging was
a sleeve of four hundred Marlborough Lights. What the
fuck? But what was this? A note:

> *Hi Whisky,*
> *Hope all is well. Am enjoying life on the outside.*
> *Thought I would send you a little pressie.*
> *No Mayfairs or any of that shite.*
> *Special Cigarettes.*

Take care,
Scary.

Was this some sort of bloody joke? Cigarettes. There wasn't even a full sleeve here. It looked like he'd helped himself to a packet, as the cellophane was ripped off. I opened the carton and took a pack out. The cellophane on the packet had been removed too. I opened the box and took out a cigarette. It looked like a regular old Marlborough, smelled like one too. What the fuck? I looked at my letter. It was postmarked the tenth of November (one week ago). I opened it up and leaned back to read.

Whisky,

Firstly, let me say that I am sorry to hear about Brian, and even sorrier that you had to find him like that. I can't believe how horrible that must have been. Secondly, I appreciate your apology about the nastiness of your previous letter. You're right, it was well out of order.

I find it odd however that you chose to tell me those things right before you admitted that you hadn't actually got any savings. Were you hoping that it would stop me getting angry? If so then you are very much mistaken. I AM VERY ANGRY. I cannot believe that I have been working my arse off all summer, saving every penny I could, while you haven't saved a single thing. What a mug you must take me for. Well I've got news for you mister, I'm not going to stand for it any more.

I have been thinking seriously about where our relationship is going and have come to a few decisions. I will be on camp on the 17th November. I start work at five o' clock in the evening. Meet me at four o' clock outside The Irish bar. We need to talk, face to face.

Rachael.

Jesus, I was twenty minutes late already. That wasn't going to go down too well. I was already in the dog house and now I was going to be at least twenty five minutes late for our first meeting in nine months. I snatched my coat from the bed, seized a pack of the Marlborough's and darted out the chalet door, before sprinting over towards the Irish bar.

The path under the tunnel was a little icy, forcing me to slow down as I passed under it, for safety's sake. At the other side I picked up the pace and thundered through the car-park full of coaches and police. As I did so I must have alarmed one of the police dogs, because it began barking ferociously at me as I approached. The handler glared at me with a suspicious look, as though I were running up to attack him. I undid my coat, flashing my uniform at him and said 'Sorry, didn't mean to alarm it, I'm just late for work.'

He stared impassively, and I accelerated away again, praying that she would still be there when I got there.

Chapter 42

Thank the lord she was there, though she didn't look too happy.

'Hi Rach,' I said, breathlessly.

'Hello,' came the cold reply.

'Sorry I'm late. I literally just got your letter now. You're lucky I read it straight away.'

'Lucky? I don't know about that, I was just about to go. Maybe that would have saved me from your excuses and lies.'

'What lies? Come on. I haven't seen you for nine months. Don't you have a hug for me?' I asked, advancing towards her with my arms open.

'No,' she said, folding her arms and backing away, her body language defensive to say the least. 'I just wanted to meet up so that we can say goodbye, properly. Like I've been saying in my letters, I don't intend to be working in this shitty business for the rest of my life. I've made my mind up. I'm definitely going to Australia, I booked my flights this week.'

'When are you flying?'

'On the third of January.'

'Who else is going with you? Taylor?'

'No!' she said, a little too quickly. 'I'm going alone.'

'Alone! Bullshit. You're going with him, aren't you?'

'I've told you, no.'

'I don't believe you. Who goes to Australia on their own?'

'Thousands of people.'

'Yeah, blokes.'

'Women too, you wanker. I came to this shit hole on my own, and I went to Tenerife on my own too.'

'Yeah, and you had a place to stay and a job already sorted out, when you came here didn't you? Where do you plan to stay in Australia?'

'Hostels. That's where backpackers stay. It's a good way to meet new people.'

'New blokes you mean?'

'Stop fucking making me out to be obsessed with blokes. I don't need a bloke to keep me happy. I'd be perfectly happy to stay single.'

'Yeah, that way you'd be able to shag around.'

'Right. That's it. I've had enough. I've told you what I'm doing, now goodbye, and have a nice life,' she said turning around and walking away.

'No! Wait. Please Rach,' I yelled, grabbing her shoulder and spinning her around. 'Let me come with you. Please. I want to go to Australia.'

'Ha! That's a good one. How you gonna get to Australia? Cycle? You need money to go to Australia you know. You need two thousand pounds at least, just to get a work visa.'

'I'll get the money. Please let me come with you. I'm sorry I've been acting so paranoid. It's just that I've missed you so much. While I've been rotting away in this shit hole, you've been out partying every night and on the beach all day. Wouldn't you be a little paranoid if that's what I did for a living?'

'There's a lot more to it than that you know. I have to look after a lot of people, most of whom need looking after, believe me. It's not like I'm lazing around on the beach all day. I've been working bloody hard, so that we could get a flat together. But you couldn't even save a few hundred quid, in nine months. What sort of future would I have with you?'

'I'll get the money together for the flat.'

'Don't give me anymore of your bullshit. Besides, I'm going to Australia now.'

'I'll come to Australia with you. It would be great.'

'It will be great. Great for me. I don't need a dead weight like you holding me back in my life. If there's one thing that going to Tenerife taught me it's that you need to keep moving forward in life. You, you're gonna be stuck working here till you die, or get sacked. It's pathetic really. You're gonna end up just like that poor old fucker that you found in the bath. As for me I don't want anything more to do with a wretched loser like you, and that's all I've got to say to you. Now goodbye.'

'You fucking cheeky bitch,' I shouted, more in hope of receiving an apology than out of any real anger, but she didn't even look back at me. She just carried on walking away.

So that was it then. That's what I had become to her. This beautiful creature that had once adored me and promised unending love and devotion now saw me as a pathetic loser, destined to die on camp. Not even a hug or kiss, after nine months of waiting for her return.

Nothing, it was as though she were switching of a light, she was so callous about the end of our relationship. The loss of self worth was all consuming. Was I really so easy to cast off, that she could do it in such a cold fashion? Evidently so. I was overcome with the sudden urge to do myself in. What was the point in my sad, pathetic little existence? Rachael was right; I was a wretched specimen indeed. There was no hope either. I was full of shit, and pipedreams. There wouldn't be any money for a flat, or Australia. There was only just enough money for a chalet and for fucking Skegness. Even this, pitiful existence would no doubt come to an end soon. With the closing of camp loomed a four month period of unemployment, punctuated only by ten day's hard slog when the camp opened for Christmas, for which I would be paid the princely sum of two hundred pounds, after tax. That's it, I thought, I'm just gonna have one last cigarette and then I'm going to Everydays to get a tub of paracetamol and a bottle of brandy.

This'll teach the bitch, I thought, as I marched towards the supermarket. I lit the cigarette and inhaled deeply. It tasted good, less woody than those fucking Mayfairs. No wonder condemned men always chose to smoke before being shot.

Then it hit me. Half way down the cigarette I was suddenly overcome by a massive constriction in my throat, forcing me into a choking fit. People turned and stared as I bent over gasping for air, but no one came to help. As I fell to my knees, placing my hands before me on the ground, desperately trying to fill my lungs with air, the most primitive instinct of all kicked in, the instinct to survive. A couple of minutes earlier I had wanted an end to it all and now I wanted nothing more than to fill my lungs with life giving oxygen. The irony was typical of the tragicomedy pantomime that was my life.

Eventually, slowly, agonisingly, the muscles in my throat began to relax again. I took a painful lung full of air, all thoughts of killing myself vanquished. What the fuck was that? An asthma attack? I had never had one before, but that's what I imagined it would feel like. Jesus, I thought, now I'm gonna have to give up smoking. I looked at the half smoked cigarette in my hand, disgusted with this latest turn of events. On the day that a batch of four hundred quality cigarettes arrives on my doorstep, I'm forced into giving up smoking. Then, looking mournfully at the Marlborough, I realised it was burning oddly, and giving off a toxic looking smoke. What the hell was this? It smelled like burning plastic. I stubbed it out and pulled the butt from the tobacco. Inside was a smouldering plastic tube, like a mini straw, the contents of which, appeared to be white powder. I realised straight away what it was. It was whiz.

Chapter 43

Despite the fact that I take drugs, I've never really considered myself to be, what my mother might call, a druggie. To me, a druggie is a heroin addict or a crack head, not someone who takes speed or ecstasy on a recreational basis. I've never even really liked drug dealers, Jo included. They are merely people that have to be tolerated in order to achieve a desired outcome, kind of like the boss at work. You pretend to like them to keep them sweet, when really you despise almost everything about them.

Becoming a drug dealer was therefore not an occupation that I aspired to. I hated the idea that, because of Scary's absence, I would be forced to pedal this fucking shit myself. How would I go about doing this? Cold calling was one option, but what would I say to random strangers? 'Here mate, wanna score?' It sounded shit. Then I remembered what Rachael had said in one of her letters about Taylor, selling gear to supplement his income.

No doubt Taylor was a bit of a user too, all low level dealers were, and things being the way they were on camp, it was safe to assume that he wouldn't have anything on him, what with the sniffer dogs and all. I bet that sly fuck was dying to score. Well I was just the man to sort him out. But first I needed to peddle my arse to medical and get myself a sick note.

...

I lied to the doctor that I had been feeling sick all morning. I knew from personal experience what the symptoms of food poisoning were and described these convincingly to the old bastard, while trying to look like I was in a considerable amount of pain.

I was fairly sure that Lorraine didn't believe me when I marched into her office with the doctor's note. She just looked at me through those thick lenses, with an expression that told me she knew I was lying. I knew that she would also have my shed 'raided' by security that night to see if I was in, resting. I was bound to be caught out, but what did it matter? This was the last weekend of the season, and soon I would be two grand richer.

Fuck her.

After leaving her office, I paid a visit to the souvenir shop, next to Everydays, where I purchased a money belt with a huge Butlins logo on it. I stuffed as many wraps of whiz as I could into the money belt and went in search of Taylor.

It took a fair bit of leg work to find out where he was stationed. I had to ask four reps if they knew a Taylor, who worked in Tenerife before I found one who did.

'Do you mean Taylor Richardson?' said the rather attractive young 18-30's rep, brushing her long auburn curls from her face, revealing a name badge, which was positioned right on top of a wonderfully voluptuous tit. 'I think he's at The Broadway.'

'Thank you very much... Charlotte,' I replied, seizing the opportunity to stare at the name badge/tit.

'You're welcome, enjoy your weekend.'

'Oh I intend to Charlotte. Thanks again.'

The Broadway eh? Perfect. Right next to the staff canteen. If anyone asked why I was wondering around camp, while I was supposed to be sick, it was because I was going to the canteen. Identifying Taylor would be easier than I thought too. The name badges were a godsend. Entering The Broadway, I bounded up the stairs four at a time, despite my imaginary affliction. Good job Lorraine wasn't around.

The place was empty, a few punters were wondering around, but most of them seemed to be scouting the place out, before the big night that lie ahead. In the far corner were two reps in uniform, one of whom appeared to be a man. I moved towards them, slowly, in case Rachael was around. I didn't want her to think I was stalking the bloke who was attempting to shag her behind my back. As I got closer the two parted, with the male rep moving in my direction. I watched him getting closer, waiting for his name badge to come into focus. And then it did, Taylor. He was tall, taller than me anyway and pretty well built, tanned of course, having spent so much time in Tenerife and a long blonde surfer style hair cut. A real pretty boy, no wonder Rachael was so fond of the conniving wanker.

'Excuse me mate, are you Taylor Richardson?'

'Yes mate, can I help you?'

'I hope so. You were based in Tenerife right?'

'Yes mate, was I your rep? Sorry, I see a lot of people, it's hard to remember everyone.'

'Yes you were my rep, you sorted me out a couple of times while I was on holiday in Las Americas.'

'Er, don't remember sorting anyone out in Las Americas,' he replied, glancing over his shoulders.

'Oh you did, and I just wanted to repay the favour. I really appreciated you looking after me over there and thought I'd chuck a bit of powder your way.'

'Sorry mate, I don't really have any money on me. Not that I'm into that type of thing anyway.' he was still guarded.

'You don't need any money Taylor. I told you, you did me a big favour out there and now I want to return the favour. It's on the house.'

He looked a little more interested now, enraptured even. Nothing like free drugs to spark the interest.

'What sort of stuff are you talking about?'

'Oh, nothing too heavy, just a bit of speed. I've got a mate who wants me to get rid of some of it for him, and he gave me quite a bit for myself. I'd be glad to chuck some your way if you fancy any.'

'And how, has your mate managed to get this past the police?'

'Easy, he works on camp. It's been here for the last few weeks, before the police arrived.'

'How much has he got?'

'About four hundred grams.'

'How much per wrap?'

'A tenner, except to you of course, I'll give you a ten wraps free.'

'Why?'

'Because you sorted me out in Las Americas.'

'I really don't remember that.'

'Well I do, and that's what's important isn't it. All I ask is that if any punters ask you where they can score, you point them in my direction.'

'That's it?'

'That's it. I'll give you five wraps now, for tonight, and five tomorrow, provided I haven't been lifted by security.'

'Pretty clued up are they?'

'Not really. Besides it's mainly 18-30's private security staff looking after the venues. The regular guys have been relegated to watching the main gates and looking after the staff club.'

'Where you gonna be?'

'That depends on where you're gonna be.'

'In here, The Broadway.'

'Well that's where I'll be too. I'll find you tonight and let you know where I'll be positioned.'

'When do I get the wraps?'

'Like I said, I'll find you tonight.' I wanted to add, 'you sly cunt,' to the end of that sentence but bit my tongue and turned to walk away. He was in the bag, all I had to do now was turn up tonight and get rid of as much speed as humanly possible, for tomorrow would no doubt bring the sack.

Chapter 44

The Broadway was rammed. Packed full of gyrating bodies, the female half of which were extremely scantily clad. This was the highlight of the year without a doubt. No Abba, no Black Lace, not a shitty house band in sight, the place was like a proper club for the first time all season. I loved it already.

I surveyed the perimeter of the club, scrutinising the place for the ideal position to set myself up. Near the toilets was the best bet. There were a few chairs, where I would be able to comfortably plonk myself while awaiting patrons to purchase my wares. This location had the added advantage of being reasonably far away from both the mad swarm that was the dance floor and the huge speakers, which would render verbal communication virtually impossible.

Having decided upon my position, I began stalking that underhand cocksucker Taylor. I eventually found him near the bar, chatting up a gullible looking blonde maiden. I watched from afar. Taylor was leaning over and talking directly into the girl's ear, when he caught sight of me lurking about fifty meters away. I nodded and he said something to the blonde before taking his leave and heading my way with a huge smile on his face.

'Good news,' he said, as he approached. 'I've already found you a customer, who wants to take twenty wraps off your hands.'

'Twenty, eh? Who's the customer?'

'One of the reps, he's planning to have a party tonight and wants to make sure he's got something to lure the girls around with.'

'Wouldn't be you by any chance would it?'

'No! What do you take me for? Besides I've got ten wraps already, haven't I?'

'You've got five for now, and you'll get another five tomorrow.'

'I've been thinking. I can get rid of this stuff for you, no sweat. Just cut me in on the profit and we'll get rid of it in one night, easy.'

'I'm not cutting anyone in on the profit. I've told you already, it's not my speed. It's a friend's and he's not gonna be too happy if I start finding him business partners is he? If you want to take it off my hands at a tenner a wrap and sell it for more then you're welcome, but I want a tenner a wrap, OK?'

'No one's gonna pay more than a tenner a wrap.'

'They'll pay. There's no choice, it's that or nothing. You got the money for your mate's twenty wraps?'

'Yeah, you want it now?'

'Can't see why not. Tell you what, come to the bogs with me and I'll sort it out. That way I can show you where I'm gonna plant myself too.'

We made our way to the toilets, where we entered a cubicle and I dug out twenty-six wraps from the money belt that I had bought earlier. Taylor counted out two hundred quid and I stuck it into the money belt before tucking it back under my shirt. I handed him twenty five wraps. Five for him and twenty for his mate, then cut out a huge line from my own wrap and invited Taylor to snort it from one end while I did from the other. He rolled up a tenner, while I used a straw I had brought especially for the job.

'Cheers,' he said wiping his eyes and nose when he had finished.

'No bother mate, after all what's mine is yours eh?' I said, sounding a little angry.

'What was that?'

'Nothing. You're welcome, come on I'll show you where I'm gonna be sitting.'

I led the way out and pointed to the spot I had picked out near the entrance to the bogs, before warning him, 'Don't send any large groups. If anyone wants a job lot, just send one of them over with the cash.'

'Yeah don't worry, if there's any big orders I might add a little to the price and make myself a bit of beer money.'

'You're more than welcome Taylor, more than welcome.'

Taylor made his way back towards the bar, where the gullible blonde was still waiting for him. I watched him whispering into her ear and she threw her head back in laughter, before looking over in my direction. What was that prick saying about me? I wondered.

...

By eleven o' clock I had sold another hundred wraps, on top of the twenty that Taylor's mate had purchased earlier. I had to hand it to Taylor, he was a decent enough pusher. He did most of the legwork himself too, so he was either adding on VAT or he was doing it to enhance his credibility as 'the man'. Being the only one able to get hold of the drugs would no doubt enhance his street cred, indeed his entourage appeared to be growing rather rapidly.

However, I was getting increasingly anxious about having over a thousand pounds stuffed into my money belt. I would be easy pickings if any of the punters Taylor sent my way decided to mug me, and I began to become more and more paranoid. Who was that last guy he sent over? He looked like a bit of a thug, tattoos all down his forearms. I was sure he'd been eyeing my money belt too. Where had he gone now? I'd lost sight of him about five minutes ago. He could be waiting for me outside for all I knew. I didn't like this shit. I wished that Taylor would do *all* the legwork, rather than just most of it.

Maybe I should have sold it on to him, cheaply and taken a cut in profits. Nah, where would he get a few thousand pounds? He'd probably do a runner with the drugs and money. Taylor was not to be trusted. I should remember that. Don't trust Taylor.

'Excuse me mate,' came a voice next to my ear, jolting me from my introspection, and making me almost leap from my chair.

'Jesus!' I said, holding my pounding heart.

The guy stood in front of me had dark hair and features that gave him a gypsyish appearance. His hands were covered in sovereign rings and he had a huge gold dog chain draped over his neck. Definitely a bit of a geezer, but slightly built enough not to look too threatening. He spoke in a high pitched cockney accent.

'Sorry boss, didn't mean to scare you or naffink. I've been sent in your direction. The rep over there says you might be able to sort me out.'

'With what?'

'He says you've got some speed. Is that all? Naffink else?'

'I haven't got anything, but I know a man with a bit of powder. That's all, nothing else. How much you want?'

'About fifteen wraps. For me and my mates.'

'Don't you want any for tomorrow?'

'I might make it twenty, I'll have to talk to the lads.'

'Well you go talk to your mates and I'll go find mine, then I'll meet you in the toilets in five minutes. Bring the money, a tenner a wrap, and I'll bring the powder.'

'OK mate, cheers.'

I entered the toilets and took position in a cubicle, where I took out twenty wraps from my money belt and put them in my pocket, ready to dig out as though they were all I had on me. I could hear a groaning coming from the cubicle next door and a slurping noise that sounded like someone was getting a blowjob next door. The noise aroused me a little, stirring my whiz shrivelled dick into a state of semi-hardness. I listened and waited.

The music suddenly became louder, then quieter again as the entrance to the toilets opened and closed. I heard coughing and shuffling feet, then the sound of the cubicle door next to me being tried, followed by a knock on it.

'Fuck off,' came a gruff sounding voice from the cubicle next door.

The door to my cubicle moved slightly. Someone was trying it, must be the geezer. Then a knock, yeah definitely him. I opened the door with a smile and was about to beckon him in when I realised it wasn't actually the geezer. It was someone else.

'You done in there mate?' he asked.

'Er, yeah, go ahead,' I couldn't exactly say no to this guy and then invite the geezer inside. Not while this poor fucker waited outside to take a shit. It was evident that the cubicle next door would be engaged for some time, so I elected to let the man use the bog. I would have to wait near the sinks for the geezer to arrive.

The music from outside became louder again. Someone else was coming in.

'Started hanging round the blokes' bogs have you? I think they call that cottaging don't they? Might have known you were as bent as your fucking roommate. Watch your backs lads, bender alert!' It was Knuckles and co, in their civvies, evidently enjoying an evening off work. They laughed loudly at his joke and barged their way past me to the urinals.

'Oi, stop staring at my fucking cock,' one of them shouted at me.

Time for a sharp exit, I thought, turning to the hand dryers. The music became louder again as the toilet doors opened and the geezer entered excitedly. I hardly had chance to warn him, before he blurted out.

'You got it then? I've got the cash.'

'Got what?' Knuckles interjected.

'Yeah, got what?' I echoed, widening my eyes at the geezer as if to say *shut the fuck up!*

'Er, nothing,' he said, a little too shiftily. 'Sorry, thought you were someone else.'

'Well I'm not. Though I wouldn't mind being at the moment,' I replied, swiftly brushing past him and attempting to tread on one of his feet as I did so. I looked over my shoulder as I opened the door and saw Knuckles eyeing me with suspicion.

He knew something was up, he fucking knew.

Chapter 45

'Right mate, I'm out of here. One of the camp's security guards is on to me.'

'Where you gonna go?'

'The Moonshiner,' I replied.

'The Moonshiner?' Taylor asked incredulously. 'Why not The Showboat?'

I couldn't really go to The Showboat, as I was supposed to be working there. I would doubtless be spotted and ejected from the place; it had to be The Moonshiner.

'Cause I fucking like The Moonshiner, OK?'

'OK, do I still get my extra five wraps?'

'Yeah, if you manage to send any large orders my way.'

Taylor looked doubtful, and rightly so, I didn't intend to give him a fucking thing.

'Why don't you come to the party afterwards? You'll probably get rid of a fair bit there.'

'I might just do that Taylor. Which chalet is it in?'

'D14, on the other side of camp.'

'Ah, the staff side, I know it well. I'll probably see you there old bean. If you get any big orders come over to The Moonshiner and you can add a few quid for yourself.'

With that I turned and left the building swiftly, hoping that Knuckles and his crew hadn't seen me. I couldn't see any of them and this made me just as nervous as being in the bogs with them. I couldn't shake the feeling that he was watching me, eyeballing me suspiciously from somewhere in the crowd.

...

The Moonshiner was just as crowded as The Broadway. Less people, but less space to accommodate them, meant that it was almost impossible to move anywhere in the venue, including the fringes. God knows what they would do in the event of a fire.

I surveyed the area, trying to figure out where Taylor might spot me if he were to come in, looking to secure some gear. I didn't hold out much hope for pushing the stuff myself. I just wasn't that good at approaching strangers. Maybe I could get them to approach me. That was it. I needed an 18-30's reps uniform. That way people would be more likely to ask me if I knew where they could score.

Genius.

Looking around for a rep I spotted one in the corner. I could only just make her out but I was pretty sure it was Rachael. Typical, the only venue I could operate in just happened to be where my recent fucking ex was stationed. I was acutely aware that I might look like a bit of a bunny boiler if she spotted me lurking in the club where she was working, especially as I was supposed to be working elsewhere. Fuck it, I thought, I had to get rid of this shit and Rachael owed me something after just dumping me out of the blue.

'Hi Rach,' I said approaching her from behind. She turned around, a perplexed across her face.

'What are you doing in here?'

'I'm enjoying my last weekend.'

'Why aren't you at work?'

'I threw a sickie.'

'A sickie! Are you joking? You mean to tell me you are going to throw away a three year reference, for the sake of a weekend?'

'Well you said I'd be here until I got the sack or died and I didn't much like the sound of the dying option, so fuck it I'll take the sack.'

'And what do you plan to do for money?'

'I plan to go work in Australia.'

'I've told you, you need two thousand pounds to get a working holiday visa, and I also told you I plan to go alone.'

'I never said I was planning to go with you. I'm gonna go with Scary Carey.'

'So where are two captains of industry like you planning to get two thousand pounds each?'

'Well I've already got one thousand two hundred in my pocket and I'll have the rest by the end of the weekend.'

'I don't believe you,' she sneered, turning her face away from me.

'Oh don't you, so what's this?' I opened up the money belt, revealing the wad that lay within.

'Where the bloody hell have you got that from? You haven't robbed a till I hope?'

'No it's from selling whiz. I've got almost another three hundred wraps to get rid of and I need you to help me.'

'I'm not selling drugs and I can't believe that you are either. Are you fucking mad? Do you want to go to prison or something? How long do you think a skinny little prick like you would last on the inside? You'd hang yourself after your first arse fucking.'

'Look, that's my risk OK, and I'm not asking you to sell any drugs for me. I just want you to get me an 18-30's uniform top, so that people might approach me asking where they can score. I'll do the rest.'

'Whisky, I want no part in this. If you want to risk prison, that's up to you, but don't ask me to help send you there.'

'Look, Taylor helped me. So why can't you?'

'Taylor! When have you spoken to fucking Taylor? How do you even know what he looks like?'

'I didn't. I just asked around and found him. He's been selling wraps for me in The Broadway.'

'Fuck me! So you're trying to get Taylor sent down too are you? Well that's just fucking great, you leave Taylor out of your crazy scams.'

'You sound more worried about him than you do about me.'

'I am. Taylor has been nothing but kind to me for the last nine months and all you've done is given me grief, about him. Do you know what? Fuck it...I slept with Taylor...last week...and you know why? Because you pestered me so much about it, that I actually went and did it, to spite you, and to prove to myself that I was over you. There. Are you happy now that you know I fucked him? That's what you wanted to know all along isn't it? Now fuck off, and leave me alone.'

I was gobsmacked. She was so cold, so clinical. There was no 'sorry', or 'it just happened, I couldn't help it'. She did it deliberately to spite me, and now she was more worried about his fucking well-being than mine. Well fuck her.

'You fucking slag!' I yelled, before turning round and barging my way out of the venue.

Outside, the cold November air hit me. So that was it, she'd fucked Taylor. Not much hope of getting rid of this stuff now. I couldn't face that weasley bastard, nor could I be bothered to sell it myself. In truth, my only motivation for getting the money together was to try to win back Rachael. There was no point anymore. I would just post the money and the speed back to Carey tomorrow, and tell him to keep it all for himself. All I wanted now was a bottle of gin and a good cry.

Chapter 46

I turned out from the entrance to The Moonshiner and suddenly realised I was already crying, wailing in fact. There were lots of punters milling around outside and I wanted to get away from them as quickly as possible, so I headed off the main promenade and walked behind The Moonshiner to follow the back path that I sometimes used as a shortcut. It was dark and there wasn't a soul around. Ideal for my purposes. I walked along as though I were drunk, ricocheting from walls and lampposts like a pinball, crying like a baby. When I reached the back of the Foodcourt, I decided to lean against the building and try to compose myself.

I let out a huge animal cry, before falling to my knees, with my arms raised to the heavens, like William Dafoe's death scene in *Platoon*.

'Why fucking me?' I screamed to the sky above. 'Why do you always fuck things up for me?'

'Because you're a faggot, that's why,' came the answer, from somewhere above me.

What the fuck? I thought looking around for the source of this celestial voice. But it wasn't a heavenly body that greeted me as I looked behind. Quite the opposite, it looked like the devil himself, manifested as an off duty security guard.

'Leave me alone will you? I can't be bothered with your insults just now.'

'Oh, I'm not here to insult you, though I might do a bit of that as well. I'm here to kick the fucking shit out of you, unless of course you just hand it over.'

'Hand what ov..AGGHHRRR,' I began to ask before being struck across the face with a massive fist.

'Don't play your fucking games with me son. I'm gonna really hurt you if you keep on,' Knuckles spat as he grabbed my neck and began to squeeze.

'Please,' I choked. 'I'll admit everything. Take me to Des now and I'll confess.'

He let go of my neck and circled me, as I attempted to fill my lungs with air. I tried to sit up and he kicked me in the small of the back.

'Aggghhrr…Why are you doing this? I've told you, I'll confess. Just take me to the security office and you'll have your bust. Des will love you.'

'Confess what? What you been selling?' he asked, bending over and grabbing me by the throat again. I saw no use in lying.

'Speed.'

'How much?'

'About four hundred grams.'

'Where you got it stashed?'

I delayed, a little too long and he cut my air supply off again, before repeating the question. 'I said, where you got it stashed?'

'Here, round my waist.'

'Huh,' he said, laughing as he removed my money belt and began rummaging through the contents. 'You're even dumber than I thought, keeping it all on you.'

'Yeah well, you got me now. You win. I don't even care anymore,' I ranted, as Knuckles quickly counted the money. And I didn't. I couldn't give a flying fuck. I just wanted him to stop hitting me. I had lost Rachael and would now forfeit my job and probably my liberty, but all I cared about was not being strangled or punched again by this savage.

'Come on then, let's get this over and done with,' Knuckles said, when he finished counting. He smiled and held out his left hand to help me from the floor. I took it, eager to get off the wet gravel and he started to pull me up. As I was almost standing I saw his smile change into a snarl and just had time to see the right hand as it formed into a fist, right before it smashed into the side of my skull.

I attempted to protect my head as the blows rained in and think I managed to crawl into the foetal position as a series of thuds and flashes became my only sensations beside fear. Then, eventually, sweet, sweet darkness wrapped itself around me.

Chapter 47

'Hello mate,' came the voice beside me. I looked around but couldn't see where it came from. Everything looked blurred and I strained to get things in focus, but couldn't. 'Do you need another pillow?'

I didn't know. Did I need another pillow? Why would I need another pillow? I wasn't comfortable, that's for sure, but whether it was because I needed another pillow I didn't know.

'I'll get you another pillow,' said the voice, before I heard its owner shuffle of into the distance. Then darkness again.

...

'Whisky. It's me. I'm here Whisky, it's all going to be all right. You're gonna be fine,' I still couldn't see the speaker, but knew it was a different one, it was a sweet voice, female maybe.

Of course I'm gonna be all right. Why wouldn't I be? I felt fine, never been more relaxed, I thought. I felt a hand on my head, stroking me softly and I smiled and embraced the blackness once more.

...

'How you doing mate?' You're looking better today. Healing nicely I'd say.'

'Healing nicely,' I heard myself repeat.

'Yes mate, you're healing nicely. Rachael's gonna be pleased when she sees you. She's gonna be well chuffed.'

'Well chuffed,' I repeated again, yawning.

'Yes mate, she'll be well chuffed. You get yourself back to sleep.'

'Gonna go back to sleep.'

. . .

'Wakey, wakey Paul. You've got visitors. Come on, try to sit up.'

I struggled to open my eyes and was able to make out three blurred figures beside me. A man and two women, one of whom was dressed in blue.

'Come on Paul, let's get you up,' said the woman in blue, pulling my upper body as she did. 'That's it, I'm gonna leave you with your visitors, OK?'

'Thanks,' said the other woman to the one in blue.

'It's all right, if he needs anything you know where to find me.'

I sat there, eyes closed, feeling dizzy and nauseous from being sat up. It took a while before the nausea passed and I tentatively open my eyes when it did. Everything was still a little blurred but I could make out the two bodies in front of me. One of them was Scary and the other was Rachael.

'Hello mate,' said Scary. 'You're looking better everyday. You're gonna be out of here in no time.'

'Where am I? Hospital?'

'Yes mate, you've been in here for four days. You were beaten up.'

'Yeah, I was beaten up. It was Knuckles, he beat me up.'

'I know he did, the fucker. But he's been taken care of don't you worry.'

'Who's taken care of him, you?'

'It's a long story mate. What's important is that you are getting better, isn't it Rachael?'

'Yes,' she answered. 'I was really worried about you. You had a fractured skull, they weren't sure at first if you would suffer any brain damage. But apparently you are going to be OK. The police are going to want to talk to you soon, do you think you will be up to it?'

'Might as well get it over and done with. Have they got someone waiting at the hospital guarding me?'

Scary cracked up at this, 'You're not John Dillinger, you mad bastard. Why would they have someone guarding you?'

'In case I try to do a runner.'

'Why would you do that?'

'To avoid jail. For selling the whiz.'

'Look, keep your voice down OK. The police don't know about the whiz. Well they don't know about us and the whiz.'

'So why are they here?'

'Because you've been the victim of a serious assault.'

'Oh, so I'm not going to prison?'

'No, you're not going to prison, I'll let Rachael tell you all about it. I'm nipping outside for a cigarette,' he exclaimed, standing up and pulling a box of Lambert and Butler from his pocket. I watched him walk away before turning to Rachael. She was looking at me sympathetically, her huge brown eyes looked watery. She really had been worried about me. I felt a fusion of emotion and self pity well up inside me and burst into tears.

'I'm so sorry,' I sobbed, 'I've fucked everything up, and I'm so, so, sorry.'

'Yes you have fucked everything up you idiot,' she replied, dabbing her own eyes. 'Why did I ever get involved with you eh.'

'Because I've got a big dick,' I answered, half crying, half laughing.

'No you haven't. It's very average actually, but you make up for it with a fast arse.'

'Very funny,' I snivelled. 'Can I have a hug?'

'Of course you can have a hug,' she replied, advancing towards me and pulling me into her bosom. I sat there sobbing into her breast, for at least five minutes while she tightened her grip every time I wailed another apology.

'Stop telling me you're sorry Whisk. It's all forgotten about OK?'

'I just missed you so much. I hated you being away, it was worse than the beating I just took. It was nine months of utter torture. I'm thoroughly lost without you. You were the best thing that ever happened to me and I fucked it all up.'

'I'm here now. That's what matters. I'll stay here until you're better as well.'

'But then what? Then you'll be off to Australia and you'll forget all about me again. Then things will be as bad as they were before.'

'I'm not going for a while yet, and it's only a year. You can manage without me for a year can't you?'

'I don't like managing without you,' I sobbed, and she pulled me into her breast again, holding me until I composed myself. I pulled away and changed the subject from her trip.

'Anyway, how did you know that it was Knuckles who beat me up?'

'I saw him. It was after we argued in The Moonshiner, I thought you were going to do something stupid, maybe attack Taylor, so I came after you. I couldn't find you down the promenade, but when I was returning to The Moonshiner I saw Knuckles coming from behind the Foodcourt, with what looked like your moneybelt. I knew from your letter earlier in the season that you'd had a fight with him and thought it was odd that he had a money belt like the one you had just shown me. So I went behind the Foodcourt and found you there, beaten up.'

'So you found me did you? I'm sorry you had to see me like that.'

'It was awful. I thought you were dead from the amount of blood around you. I reported it to the bouncer on the door at The Moonshiner and he took care of you while the ambulance arrived. Then I came here with you in the ambulance and when the police arrived I told them that I had

seen your attacker beating you up. I told them it was a
security guard from camp called Matt. I also told them that
Matt had sold me some speed earlier that evening, and they
did the rest. They found the drugs and the money when they
arrested him on his way home. They also found a knuckle
duster, with blood on it, which is no doubt yours. I don't
think Knuckles is going to get out for a couple of years.'

'You clever bugger. So I've got you to thank for me not
going to jail have I?'

'No, you've got Knuckles to thank for that. If he had just
taken you to Des and handed you in you would have been
fucked. But the greedy bastard thought he'd seen his chance
to line his pocket and took it. He could still have been OK, if
he had dumped the speed and kept the cash, but I guess he
thought he could offload it. So in a way he *was* planning to
deal drugs, and his punishment will be just.'

'I don't want to be around here when he gets out, I can tell
you.'

'Well that won't be for a while yet, and besides, I think
you'd be lucky to have your job next season anyway.
Throwing a sickie on your last weekend and then being
found getting beaten up by a drug dealer. How do you think
that looks to the management? It looks as though you are
somehow implicated. Luckily the police can't prove
anything about you. When they question you, it would be
wise to tell them that you owed him money for some speed
he had sold you, fifty quid or something. That way it looks
like it's for personal use, yet enough money for him to beat
you up.'

'You've really thought about this haven't you?'

'Well, I've spent four days in a hospital with an
unresponsive boyfriend, I've had a lot of time to think.'

'You said boyfriend. Does that mean we're back together?'

'We'll see what happens. I'm not promising anything, just yet. But I was worried I would lose you for a while, and I realised that I still love you despite your many, many flaws.'

'I love you too. More than anything in the bloody world.'

'I know you do. Oh, here comes Scary. I'm gonna nip out for a cig myself. I'll leave you to talk with him.'

I watched her recede to the door where she spoke with Scary. He handed her a cigarette from his pack and his lighter before turning and coming over to the side of my bed.

'Looks like you're patching things up there mate.'

'Yeah, sort of. Look mate I owe you an apology.'

'What for?'

'Losing the money and the drugs. I blew it. Your plan to get us both to Australia, I fucked it all up.'

'You didn't fuck it up, Knuckles did. That cockhead blew it for us, but it's almost worth a few grand to see him end up in prison.'

'Yeah, but, you've lost your job and now you don't even have the money to get to Australia anymore. I can't believe he managed to mug us both.'

'He didn't mug me, he just beat me up.'

'He told me he took the money from you.'

'Well obviously not, as you found it buried where I told you.'

'Yeah but I thought he'd taken the two hundred quid from you.'

'What two hundred?'

'Look I know about the extra two hundred mate. I'm not bothered, you took the risks, I don't blame you for keeping a couple of hundred for yourself.'

'I don't know what you're talking about. I took a grand like I planned to, no more, and I buried it where you found it.'

'But Lorraine told me that there was twelve hundred missing from your till.'

'Did she now? And who cashed the till up I wonder?'

'Lorraine. She told me.'

'Well, I guess Lorraine saw her chance too, thieving bitch.'

'Do you think?'

'Definitely. That's Butlins mate, it's full of thieves. Everyone on camp is on the make in some way or another. Remember when Mark Smith got caught a couple of years back? There was a scandal, the longest serving bar manager, fiddling the safe. No one saw that one coming. I bet Lorraine's got her hands in the safe somehow too.'

'Huh, can't trust anyone these days. Anyway, I am sorry for fucking up the Australia dream.'

'Look mate, it's not been fucked up, just put on hold, that's all.'

'Yeah, permanently on hold. Where'd you plan to get a couple of grand from? You don't even have a job anymore.'

'Ever heard of the criminal injuries compensation board?'

'No, what's that?'

'That my friend is a trust that awards money to people like you and me, who have been injured as a result of a criminal act. My solicitor reckons I'm looking at about four grand for my little beating, I bet you'll be on about the same if not more, a fractured skull, that's serious man.'

'You've got a solicitor?'

'Yes, and you'll get one too, legal aid and all that. I'm telling you mate we're looking at more than we would have gotten from the sale of the drugs, much more.'

'Fucking hell! When do we get the money?'

'Well, that's the problem you see. It can take up to a year.'

'A year! What the fuck are we gonna do in the meantime? Neither of us is gonna be welcome back on camp, and we're probably blacklisted from every Butlins in Britain. What do you propose we do until next November?'

'Well, I've been meaning to talk to you about that....'

Chapter 48

Hiya Whisk,

Well, I finally made it to Australia and guess what? It's pissing it down. I've been searching all day for a job, but still haven't had any luck. The precious savings are already taking a bit of a kicking (or at least it seems that way after the relative in-expense of Thailand). I have found an apartment, which I am sharing with two Swedish girls and a Canadian called Dan. They are all really nice and Dan has offered to try and get me a job at the bar he works in, which is good of him.

There's not much else to report really. I assume you've received my postcards from Thailand, so you'll know what a great laugh Ko Samui is. I've put the address of the apartment above so you can finally write back to me. I can't wait until your compensation comes through and you fly over here, it'll be great.

Hope this letter reaches you before you start the new job, if not I guess your mum will forward it on to you.

All my love, missing you loads,

Rachael xxx

P.S. Remember it's only for a few months. I will not be impressed if you balls this new job up. I will not be impressed at all. Keep your head down please and don't fuck up!

Cheeky so and so, I thought as I placed the letter back into my suitcase. Always expecting the worst. What made her think I would balls this job up?

It was the third time I had read the letter today, and probably about the ninety second since it arrived five days ago. I didn't trust this cunt Dan, not one fucking bit. I was careful not to mention any of this in my reply however, not after the debacle over Taylor. No, better to keep shtum about my thoughts on this sly bastard.

I let out a huge sigh and began to unpack my suitcase. I could hear Scary whistling in the next room, it sounded like Ultranate's *You're Free*. Yes I *was* free, I thought, at least I was free. Things could have ended up a lot worse.

I let out another sigh and exited the tiny room, switching off the naked light bulb that hung from the ceiling on my way out. I knocked on the flimsy door next to mine and called through to Scary.

'What time you start work mate?'

'Five o' clock,' Scary replied. 'What about you?'

'In ten minutes, I'm gonna get off.'

'All right mate, good luck.'

'Yeah, cheers.'

Outside the clouds looked ominous and the wind battered the few brave souls that were wandering around camp. I zipped up my fleece and put my head down into the wind. Another sigh and I made my way over towards the staff canteen.

The canteen was empty, not surprisingly as dinner would not be served for another hour and a half. I wasn't here to eat, I was here to work. I was evidently a reject from the interview stage, not the sort of person that they wanted customers to see.

Magic.

But then again, this was Pontins, maybe things were different here. Maybe the principles that applied at Butlins were not relevant at Pontins. I dreamed of a canteen staffed entirely by buxom wenches and myself, where the finest culinary delights were served up to grateful employees who would applaud and cheer 'Bravo chef, bravo'. But having seen the state of the chalets I was fairly sure that things were going to be awfully familiar and I braced myself to be trained up in the kitchen by some manner of umpa lumpa.

I walked up to the counter and introduced myself to the blotchy looking cleaner, who was sweeping around the tables.

'Hi, I'm looking for Andy, the supervisor for the staff canteen,' I told it.

'Andy, yesh I'll jusht go and get him for you. Shit down a minute, I won't be a shecond.'

Oh god, I thought, so this is where I would be spending the next six to nine months. Great plan Scary, great fucking plan. Still I bet that bastard was pissing himself, after all he'd somehow landed the role of bar tender in the bar next to the swimming pool. All that semi naked flesh he would be looking at seemed like paradise compared to my lot.

Roll on that compensation.

Andy came out, wiping a sweaty hand down his trouser legs before extending it to shake mine.

'Hi Paul, pleased to have you on board. I've just been looking through your CV, which personnel forwarded on to me. I see you have got a bit of kitchen experience.'

'Yes a little bit.'

'And you worked at Butlins for a few years too did you?'

'Yep, hope that's not a problem.'

'Why would it be a problem?'

'Well, competition and all that. It's kind of like playing for Manchester United and then getting a transfer to Man City, isn't it?'

'Is it? I can't say I've ever thought about it like that. So why'd you leave Butlins?'

'Er, I fancied a fresh challenge.'

'And Butlins is the only experience you have in a kitchen?'

'Well mainly, but I also worked in an American bar and restaurant for a short while.'

'Oh really, which one?'

I told him TGI Fridays, but I didn't mention that it was just for three weeks. Better to make it look like I was a steady employee.

'Really, what a coincidence. We have another cook in here who used to work there. He started last week.'

'Yeah, well as you know, they have a lot of stores around the country, it's not that much of a coincidence really.'

'Yes, you're right. I'm sure there's hundreds of people working for them. Anyway, come with me and I'll show you around the place.'

I followed him into the kitchen, where around twenty cooks were busy preparing the hearty fare that would be served up to the staff in an hour or so.

'This station here is where all the salads are prepared,' he informed me. 'This is the walk in fridge, where we keep the raw meats and this...'

I've no idea what he said next because what I saw in the corner of the kitchen stopped me in my tracks. Unfortunately he had seen me too and was advancing towards me with a strange twisted smile on his face. He looked *really* happy to see me, which made him look all the more injurious to me.

'Ah, here's the chap I was telling you about,' began Andy. 'Paul I'd like you to meet Moussa, he used to work for TGI Fridays too. Moussa I'd like you to meet Pa..'

I was already gone, pushing my way past the cleaner with the shpeech impediment and almost breaking my neck as I slipped on his wet floor. Do these knob heads not use wet floor signs? I thought. Behind me I could hear the

commotion in the kitchen. I'm not sure what Andy was
shouting but Moussa's words were pretty clear: 'I kill, I kill.'
Or some shit like that.

871330

Made in the USA